Vivid characters spice up the life of 'J

Mary Reilly
By Valerie Miner
Doubleday, 263 pp., $18.95

By Jane Smiley
Special for USA TODAY

In Valerie Miner's new novel, *Mary Reilly*, the scene is Victorian England, a much-plowed field, and the subject is Dr. Jekyll and Mr. Hyde, a book that few people may have actually read, but many know the gist of. To Miner's credit, she manages to turn up some "features of interest," as Sherlock Holmes used to say.

Mary Reilly is Dr. Jekyll's parlormaid, a woman who has survived an appallingly cruel childhood, learned to read and write, and found security and

By Thomas Victor

MINER: The servant's voice is author's great triumph.

pleasure in her routine of work in Jekyll's wealthy and well-ordered house. Miner's great triumph in the novel is Mary's voice, as she composes her sto-

ry. It is convincingly the voice of a poorly educated but intelligent servant, whose experience of the world has given her a melancholy, but bravely pragmatic turn of mind.

When she learns of the death of her mother, she writes, "All the afternoon I could think of nothing but Marm, who may be left on her mattress until I can come for her, or else turned out into some storage place so that her room can be let at once, and also I thought, now I am an orphan, for I have no one in the world who knows me."

It is not just that the diction is right, and consistent, too, but that the rhythm is right, the ex-

periences are believable, and the insights are fresh. And Mary's work is well portrayed. The invisible life of those ghostly servants who flit through almost all of British literature is vividly revealed. Mary is a remarkable character.

The Jekyll-and-Hyde plot is one of those good ideas that energizes the novel at first, then limits it later, as the characters outgrow it. Mary's fondness for her "master" is reminiscent of *Jane Eyre*, as is Jekyll's growing interest in the judgments and opinions of his servant, but, of course, any love ending is doomed. The fact that there can be no happy ending is what marks this as a modern novel — the boundaries of class cannot be crossed, nor can the damage of a brutalized child-

Mary Reilly

By Valerie Martin

Mary Reilly

VALERIE MARTIN

Doubleday   New York   London   Toronto   Sydney   Auckland

Frontispiece: *Servant.* Ambrotype by an unidentified photographer. From *Victorian Working Women* by Michael Hiley. Copyright © 1979 by Michael Hiley. Reprinted by permission of David R. Godine, Publisher.

PUBLISHED BY DOUBLEDAY

a division of
Bantam Doubleday Dell Publishing Group, Inc.
666 Fifth Avenue, New York, New York 10103

DOUBLEDAY and the portrayal of an anchor
with a dolphin are trademarks of Doubleday,
a division of Bantam Doubleday Dell
Publishing Group, Inc.

Library of Congress Cataloging-in-Publication Data

Martin, Valerie.
    Mary Reilly / Valerie Martin.—1st ed.
        p.   cm.
    ISBN 0-385-24968-3
    I. Title.
PS3563.A7295M37   1990
813'.54—dc20   89-38313
                                                                              CIP

The text of this book was set in the typeface Fournier by Crane Typesetting Service, Inc., West Barnstable, Massachusetts. The display was set in Governae by Photo Lettering Inc., New York, New York.

Designed by Marysarah Quinn

To the memory of two beloved seafarers
JRM and RLS

Acknowledgments

The author would like to thank the many friends and colleagues who helped with the preparation of this manuscript, among them Chris Wiltz, Heather Henderson, Bill Sharpe, Ann Jones, Frank Reilly, O'Neil Denoux, Bob Hosmer, Adrienne Martin, Marianne Velmans, Fiona Burtt, Nan A. Talese, Nikki Smith, and, especially, James Ellis.

Mary Reilly

*I*t wasn't the first time I'd been shut up in the closet, if closet isn't too grand a word for the little cupboard under the stairs. I was ten and small for my age, but I had to fold myself up into a painful crouch to fit into the narrow, dirty space and that was always part of the struggle, getting me to fit, which was part of his pleasure I've no doubt.

That time I didn't struggle but tried to get in place as quick as I could. He was in a rare temper and I feared he'd have my life if I didn't look sharp about doing as he said. I'd broken a cup, trying to wash it, and then hidden the pieces, which he'd found of course, so besides being a careless, loutish girl, I was a liar too and probably a thief. Marm was at her work so there was no hope of help there, not that she ever dared cross him but sometimes when she was about he went easier on me. He'd slapped me once and pulled me about by my hair before he lit on the cupboard. When he opened the door, shoving and shouting at me, I crawled in as best I could, eager to be out of his hand's reach, and as I was folding myself up so that he could close the door I caught his eye and my heart sank for I saw the ease of my punishment didn't please him and he'd had a glance of the silly figure he cut, a grown man taking on a child, and this had redoubled his anger and there would be hell to pay for me.

Then it was dark and no air. I screamed because I couldn't help it. I heard him pull out the chair at the table and take his seat there, guarding me. "Please," I begged, "let me out. I won't ever be so wicked again."

But he didn't make a sound and that made me anxious as it meant he were thinking. I put my forehead against my knees and tried not to scream or beg as I knew when he was quiet like that it would do me no good.

Then I heard him get up and leave the room. I heard the door to the alley behind open and then close. I pushed at the cupboard door but it was hopeless— there was a good lock on it, the only one in our two rooms that kept anything in or out, worse luck for me. I thought he might have gone out to the gin palace and

I set myself to a good long wait, possibly until Marm came back, so long that the thought of it brought tears · to my eyes.

But after a little while I heard him come back in, pull out the chair and sit again. "Sir," I called out, "may I please be let out now."

For answer I heard that low, sick laugh he had sometimes, when he'd had so much liquor he didn't remember the next day what he'd done, and it make me tremble as I knew this meant the very worst for me. I wished I had not spoken, to remind him I was still at his ease.

After a few minutes I heard him get up again and come to the door. Then he was standing in front of it, laughing in that way I could hardly bear to hear, and I didn't know what to do, beg or be silent. He said, "Mary, I'm opening this door, but if you know what's good for you, you'd best not move." The door opened and the light from the lamp confused me so I couldn't see. Then he leaned towards me and I saw he had a little hopsack bag with a string drawn at the top. Perhaps there was a few inches between my knees and my head, for I was looking up at him, trying to think what I had best do, but before I could make out much of anything he'd stuffed the bag in with me, saying, "Here's summat to keep you company," and then the door was closed again.

There was another black moment while I tried to understand what it was I had to fear next. I knew at once that there was something in the bag, that it was meant to harm me, but what it was my childish imagination couldn't conjure. Then I felt it moving and knew it was some animal, no doubt as frightened as I was. I'd only a thin skirt on, which I had pulled down over my knees as best I could, so it wasn't long before the creature began to work its way through the two thin layers separating us in that narrow, breathless space. I felt a claw sink into my thigh and I pulled myself up rigid, as if I could make more room, but there was no more room to make and I think the rat sensed that as well as I. I knew it was a rat and where he'd got it. There was plenty to be had in the alleys nearby and often enough he'd brought me to whimpering by sending me out for a pint when it was dark and I had to pick my way among them.

So he'd put one of these rats in the bag and closed it up with me.

I could not speak, but I tried just to breathe and then I said, "Sir, don't do this," but I had only a whispering voice so he mayn't of heard me. The rat wasn't in a panic yet, but was at gnawing the cloth and I could hear it and knew in no time the bag would give out and my own skin would be next. I threw my weight against the door so I got one arm free a little and tried to push the bag down to my feet. I cried out "Sir," and I heard him laugh again. The cloth was giving way—I could hear it and feel the animal's snout moving against my leg, but of course I could see nothing and scarcely move, so I was helpless.

I screamed. I felt the first bite at my ankle and I screamed for all I was worth, but after that I felt very little and only screamed because I could not stop screaming. Once it was out of the sack the creature was everywhere at once, crazy to get at me or away from me, I couldn't tell which, and it could move about freely as I could not. I scraped and tore my arms against the walls trying to protect myself with my hands and that is why, as you observed, many of the scars is on my hands.

After a long time in which I screamed and begged so that you would have thought a stone would be moved to pity, the door opened and the rat leaped out, scrambled across the floor to the door and back to the safety of the alley.

Or that is how I imagine it must have happened for I did not know at the time, nor did I know anything or anyone for some time to come, including my own marm who was so took when she come home and found me lying for dead in the corner with him asleep at the table that she did what I'd never have thought she had the courage to do—she called the constable and had me conveyed to the hospital at C_____ where I lay in a swoon for many weeks.

This is the account I wrote for my master nearly a year ago, six months after I took up my post as underhousemaid here. I did so at his request, attending on those details which I thought would bring the incidents to life for him. I had sketched them to him the evening when he first remarked the scars on my hands.

It was a wonder to me that Master noticed my scars, as I was on my knees blacking the grate and black to my elbows, but he is an observant gentleman and perhaps he had noticed them some earlier time. He was sitting across the room from me in his leather reading chair, not even facing me but turned to one side and absorbed, so I imagined, in perusing some scientific treatise. I was at my work, wanting to finish up quickly, as I knew he'd be wanting the fire and also I don't like to do such work before Master, but he'd come in while I was at it and so I was obliged to finish.

I was getting up my brushes and blacking when, completely unexpected by me he said, "Mary, I notice you have some scars on your hands, and others near your ear, just there." (I had reached up to touch the mark on my neck, leaving it, no doubt, smeared with black.) "Would you let me examine them, please."

I was struck dumb, too terrified to move. I can remember now, though it seems a long time ago, even another time from what I am in now, that my first thought was to run.

But where, I thought, do you run from such a civil request from your own master. Yet I could not, I knew, do as he requested for shame of my dirt, and of myself, to be looked at by a gentleman, though I reminded myself he was a doctor and might have only a professional curiosity which he'd a right and reason to gratify. So I stood up very slowly, thinking hard at it all the while, rubbing my hands in my apron, wringing my hands in shame, and I said, "Sir, I'm ashamed to come close to you as I'm so black and it do travel no matter how I might try to keep it from you."

He didn't say a thing for a moment but closed his book and sat looking at me with such a patient, kind, thoughtful look, such as I would never expect nor even want from a gentleman, until I was fair in suspense for his next words. "Go and wash, then," he said, "and come back when you feel you can approach me."

I wanted to cry out, Ah sir, that will never happen in this life, but it wasn't my place to describe to him my place, if you see what I mean, and I told myself this sharp, that his request was not unreasonable and only my own cowardice might keep me from satisfying it. All this was crowding my head, but I did manage to say "Yes, sir," and scurry off down the stairs to the kitchen where I boiled the kettle and washed me as vigorous as a new bride. There was no mirror but Mr. Poole had set out a bit of silver to be polished in the morning, so I took up one of the trays and scrubbed my face, making sure there was no black. Then I tucked my hair up in a fresh bonnet and changed my apron. My sleeves had a bit of black at the edges, so I rolled them back.

Mr. Poole had gone off to his room and Annie was already up in our attic, so I had the big, quiet kitchen to myself. It was cold, as the stove was out, yet I didn't feel anxious to return to the drawing room where Master sat waiting for me. How could I speak to him, especially on the subject he had proposed?

So I stood for a moment, letting the cold and quiet sink in and remembering my place, as Mrs. Swit used to say we mun do when we feel uncertain, and she was right on that for I begun to be calm and, seeing I had nothing to fear, went up to Master with a good will.

When I come in he'd lit the fire himself and was standing looking into it, nor did he turn to look at me, so I went right up until I was beside him, made a curtsy to get his attention and said, "Sir?"

He turned to me, slow, I thought, as if he was having a conversation with someone else and must attend to it to the last, and he looked at me close, as if it were of some interest that I should be there at all. This made me shy so I stepped back one and said, "I've come as you asked me to, sir." Then he come to himself and remembered all about me and again I saw that kind, tender look in his eyes as he took my hands and drew me near the little table with the lamp.

I was timid and would have pulled away but he had such a manner about him, being a doctor I imagine, as seemed to make it all right, so I went along and stood very still while he held my hands near to the light.

My right hand has more marks than my left, mostly on the fleshy part of my palm, then down around to my wrist. These he examined carefully, moving my thumb back and forth and tracing the thick white track there with his forefinger. While he was looking at my poor

hands I took the chance to look at his, and a more re-
fined, gentlemanly hand I think I've never seen. His fingers are long and delicate, almost like a lady's, and the
nails is all smooth and trimmed evenly, so I thought
here are hands such as should never know work, and I
wanted to hide my own rough red hands away.

"These go very deep here," he said, pressing near
my thumb. "Yet you have full use of your fingers."

"I do now, sir," I said. "For a while I could not get
that thumb to working but it come back. When the
weather's changing I know it, but other than that I'm
none the worse."

"Let me see your neck," he said.

I turned my head and pushed my hair up, though
it wasn't really necessary as the cap held it in place
pretty well. Master bent his eye upon the marks near
my ear very intent for some minutes until I was wishing
this would be all over and I could go off to my bed. I
knew what was coming but not why, so I was puzzled
and worried, but I stood still and said nothing until Master spoke.

"These appear to be teeth marks," he said. "Doubtless the bites of some animal."

"That's right, sir," I replied. "And so they are."

He touched the four marks that is close on my ear
and his fingers was that cool and soft, I closed my eyes
for a second, as I felt the blood rushing to my face. But
Master didn't notice my state. He drew his hand away
and stepped back so I recovered myself a little, but I
could not look at him when he spoke.

"Judging from the size and shape of these marks, I'd say the animal was a rodent and rather a large one."

"He were a big enough rat, that's true, sir," I said, "though I never saw him. He was heavy as a dog."

He made a sound I thought was a laugh so I looked up and found I was right, for he had still the traces of a smile about his mouth, though it was a quick one and gone already. Still his eyes smiled at me, but not with malice, so I felt bold to speak.

"Have I said something funny, sir?" I asked.

"Not what you said, Mary, but how you said it. You have a frank manner that is not without charm."

"I try to speak honest, sir," I said, "as I've nothing to hide."

"That's as it should be, Mary," he replied. Then he turned and went back to the fire where he stood with his back to me and his hands clasped behind. I waited in fair suspense, smoothing my apron like a schoolgirl. Then, as he seemed not disposed to say more, I asked, "May I go now, sir?"

Without turning to look at me he begun to talk, as if he was telling the fire about his concerns. "Yesterday," he said, "as I was passing in the hall I noticed you were working in the library, Mary."

"I was, sir," I said. "Only dusting it out."

"Well, I looked in but you didn't see me."

"No, sir," I replied, not seeing the trap I was being led into, "I did not."

"No," he continued. "You didn't because you were standing at the shelf looking into a book."

I could hardly speak, so shocked I was to be caught out and ashamed too. But I found my voice and said, "Oh, sir, I do apologize. It was a book that was lying open and I couldn't help but look into it and then when I saw what it was I did stop to read a page or two."

"And what book was it, Mary?" he said.

I thought this was hard as I knew he knew what book it was, as he had left it open, there being no one else in this house as would be looking into his books. "It were a history sir," I said, "of the kings and queens."

"And what did you think of it?"

"I thought it was a most interesting book, sir, and so well writ that I was distracted from me duties and caused you to be displeased, so now I don't think so well of it."

He turned to me then and I saw that he was still mightily amused at something, which put me off as I was struggling not to burst into tears from the quizzing and didn't see any humour in it.

"I'm not the least displeased with you, Mary," he said. "I'm delighted to have a housemaid who can not only read but be distracted by Macaulay's style."

"I can read well enough, sir," I said, "and I do whenever I can, but servants' fare is mostly high-life novels, so I'm no student and have no way of judging what's good or bad except as it pleases me."

"And you can write as well, I suppose."

"Of course, sir," I said.

"Then I want you to write something for me, Mary," he said. "Will you do that?"

"If it's in my power I will try, sir, though I fear you'll find my way of writing too mean to be of interest."

"I'll bear with that," he replied. "I want you to write me an account of the manner in which you came by this rodent. That you could be so badly bitten and not have seen the animal has piqued my curiosity."

"It was in a closet, sir, and it was black as Egypt, that's all the mystery there is to that."

"And why were you in a closet, Mary?"

"It were a punishment, sir."

He took in his breath a little, as if I'd said something that confirmed him in his thought. "Write it out for me, then, Mary. As you can," he said. "And bring it to me here tomorrow evening, so that I may read it at my leisure."

"I'll do my best, sir," I said.

"Good, then. I know you will." He turned back to the fire and took up his fire-gazing, which he does more than any man I've ever seen. The fireplace in our drawing room is a big one and puts out enough heat to roast a haunch in my view, but Master is thin-blooded, as gentlemen are I suppose, and don't mind the heat. I stood there watching him, thinking how odd it was that he should want me to write on my own history, but I couldn't find any harm in it and already I was thinking just how to start that would make it interesting to him. Then I come to myself and said, "Sir, may I go now?" and he said, "Yes," without moving a muscle but his mouth, so I ran out of the room and along the hall to the back stairs. Then I went up to the attic very slow, as if I didn't want to get to the top, milling over the whole business.

I'd have to get up an hour early as there would be no time to sit during the day, though I thought I might get in a little at tea if Mr. Poole didn't come up with some errand or chore, as is often the case. At last I got to the room, undressed in the dark and climbed in with Annie, who was dead asleep and didn't even know I was there.

I lay thinking about Master, who was down below me in his drawing room, gazing at the fire no doubt and thinking Lord knows what. Then I fell on thinking of his cool fingers against my neck, which was a thought I knew I had no business to be entertaining and I gave myself a talking to on the subject of a servant's foolishness and how wrong it is ever to have fancies outside one's station as it always leads to misery, as I've observed myself often enough, and in the midst of lecturing myself I fell asleep.

*I*t was hard to get up the next morning because it was so rainy and dark, but I knew I had my writing to do and with the rain there would surely be no time to do it during the day as Mr. Poole is always in a state when it rains (which is much of the time) and seems to have a passion for sending those under him out into it and then fussing if a bit of mud comes in the door. So I got myself out of bed and wrote up my story as best I could. Annie woke up and spoke to me in the dark (I was working by candle as we've no lamps in our room) but I told her I was just at my journal, which I do keep for my own pleasure, so she thought little of it and went back to sleep. Annie is a good girl and a hard worker, but I believe her health is not good as whenever we've a free moment she is asleep and seems to have no life but working and sleeping, which is sad.

All day I had heavy work: carried up coal and water, scrubbed the kitchen floor out on my knees, cleaned the pantry, polished the silver Mr. Poole had left out and took up the rugs in his parlour, but couldn't hang them out for the rain. So I took them all and hung them in the backyard where there's an overhang, and while I was beating them I saw Master cross the yard to his laboratory, his head down and his shoulders slumped as if he was being trod on by the rain.

I was behind the carpet, so he didn't notice me, though I kept beating at it, making a thudding sound. Yet he didn't look my way. When I saw him I thought I might sing out that I'd done as he asked and would bring it along in the evening, but many other thoughts, and something about the worried, tired look of Master as he hurried along to be at his work (which Mr. Poole says is very scientific and important, not like a common doctor who sets bones and tells sick folks they mun stay in bed, for Master sees no one and is interested in the cause of things, not how to tinker and mend, as Mr. Poole says), something in all this kept me quiet and I even stopped my beating to watch him go by. He let himself in with a key (we are none of us ever allowed in Master's laboratory and sometimes I think we should be as surely it must need a cleaning such as he cannot do himself), but just before he went in he stopped and looked back towards the house with a look so sad, as if there was something there he was leaving and he wished he never had to go. He looked all up and down the house, but not at me as I was off to the side in the overhang where the two wings come together, and then he went in and closed the door.

So I worked all day with the thought of giving my writing to Master in the evening like the promise of a fine day out before me and I thought over my writing to see had I left anything out or said anything too crudely so that he would be offended. But at dinner Mr. Poole told us that Master was taking his meal in his cabinet, as he does sometimes when he is working hard, and there would be no need to lay the fire in the drawing room, so once the dishes was put up we could all be off to bed. Mr. Bradshaw asked leave to go to his mother's in P_____ Street, as she is ill and has no one to look in on her, and so he got consent and went off directly. I sat with my beer after everyone had got up, trying to think of a way to see Master without telling Mr. Poole my reason, for though he never said it, I felt he wouldn't want Mr. Poole to know we had our conversation the night before and also Mr. Poole is very disapproving of the servants ever speaking to Master, or calling themselves to his attention in any way as he says Master should never be distracted from his work and that he is always working in his head, even when he looks like he's at rest, which is surely true.

Mr. Poole was at the sideboard making up Master's tray and complaining that he had to go into the cellar for a bottle of claret which is Master's particular favourite and Cook had served up the plate too soon so the food would be cold. I thought this were an opportunity at least to speak with Master about how I should deliver my writing so I said, "Mr. Poole, I can take the tray out now if you like and you can come behind with the claret." But he only stopped and gave me one of his cold, dead looks, like a fish's eye when you know it's none too fresh and said, "Mary, you know Dr. Jekyll forbids anyone but me to go to the cabinet door. I wonder you could forget this simple direction."

So I just ducked my head over my beer and said I was sorry but I had forgotten. After he went off I said to Cook it seemed to me someone ought to go in and clean for Master. She agreed with me and told me the side door and steps was a disgrace and every time she walked by them on the street she felt relieved that none of Master's friends knew they belonged to our house (for the corner house comes between). But I said, Master didn't have much in the way of friends that I ever saw, except his solicitor Mr. Utterson, who comes around now and then, but Cook said before I come Master sometimes gave large dinner parties and doubtless he would again when he was ready to take a rest from his work.

After we'd done up the dishes there was nothing to do but go off to bed and as it was ten and I was tired from my work I didn't mind much, but I kept wishing I had some way to deliver my writing as I promised.

Then when I was in bed, I thought mayhaps Master doesn't even remember he asked me to write out my story for him and it was just his whim at the moment so he wouldn't have to listen to me tell it and he could have some quiet in his drawing room. This cast me down very much and I went to sleep feeling tired to the bones and sad, which shows what comes of wanting to be important and feel different from others in the same station.

The next morning I was washing the front steps when Mr. Poole came out the door and spoke to me very coldly. "The Master has sent for you to come to the drawing room," he said, and I knew he was displeased and suspicious, for Master never pays much attention to the servants and hardly knows their names, or so it seems, though that may be partly due to how determined Mr. Poole is to keep Master from any bother having to do with the house and what a free rein he has over everything that goes on, including who is hired and let go. In most houses I've been in this is not the case and though I know I'm answerable always to Mr. Poole, as he is above me, still I can't help but feel that in the end I'm answerable to Master alone.

I brought my bucket in and emptied it out in the yard, then washed as best I could and put on a clean apron. My skirts was black but there was nothing to be done about that and I thought Master might not expect more from one he calls in with no more notice than he'd given me. Mr. Poole was following me about, full of disapproval and as gloomy as a cloud, but I paid him no mind. I was wondering how I would get my writing down from my room, since I felt sure it was for that Master had called me.

And so it was. As soon as I made a curtsy before him, Master put down his teacup and asked if I'd done as he requested.

"I have done it, sir," I said. "But I had no means of giving it to you, as you was in your laboratory last night."

"I see," Master said. Then he took up his tea again and sat looking into the cup as if he thought the next thing to say might be written in there. I stood it as long as I could, then I said, "I haven't got the pages on me now, sir. They're in my room and I don't like to go up there just now as Mr. Poole has his eye on me and is likely to ask what I'm about."

He gave his tea a weak smile and then I stopped being nervous for myself and noticed that he looked very unwell. His face was as pale as paper and his eyes had dark circles underneath. "And you think Mr. Poole would have some objection to your doing as I ask?" he said.

This put me in a difficulty as it could never be my place to speak ill of another servant, but particularly one like Mr. Poole who is over me and has been in this house nearly twenty years, so Cook says. "Mr. Poole would never object to anything you wished done in your own house, sir," I said, "but it's his place to tell me what you want and not the other way around."

"I see," he said, giving me his mild, amused look. "Mary, you seem to have a fairly profound view of social order and propriety."

"It's nothing extraordinary to know, sir," I said. "Every servant knows as much if he's any wish to stay in service."

"So how do you propose we solve this problem of circumventing the indefatigable Poole without compromising your position?"

"I mun tuck the pages in my sleeve after tea, sir," I said, "when I sometimes go up to my room, and then put them somewhere as you direct, so that you may pick them up at your leisure."

"You seem to have given this plan some thought," was all he said.

"Yes, sir," I said. "I have."

Then he just sat looking at me in that kind, sad way he has, but he looked so tired and ill that I felt I would ask him if he wasn't knocked up, though I wouldn't have put it that way to him. Before I could speak he said, "Will you be working in the library this afternoon?"

"Yes, sir," I said. "I'll have to dust and black the grate."

"Then you could put your pages in the book we discussed before and close it up."

"I could, sir," I said.

"Good, then," he said. "That is how we will circumvent the virtuous Poole."

I did as Master asked, but not with an easy mind. It seemed to me no good could come of it as I've never known a gentleman or lady either who would encourage one servant to deceive another. Order in a household is as important to us below stairs as above and though I have no liking for Mr. Poole, who is so vain of his intimacy with Master he seems to have no other cause to live, I could not feel easy about the way Master had spoken of him as "the virtuous Poole," showing me his contempt and taking me, whom he don't know, into his confidence. I've been in service ten years now, since I was twelve, and I've never seen such a case, though it isn't uncommon for ladies and gentlemen to play their servants off on each other and many's the husband who seeks to lay his wife low by showing his contempt for her to her own dressing maid.

After tea I looked over my writing and changed a word here or there, feeling proud of it all in all, pleased with the way I'd started out particularly, and anxious to have Master's opinion, as I have always had a great respect for those as can write things up, which is why I've kept my journal whenever I could over the years, though every time I've left a house it seems I lose them. I tucked the pages in my sleeve and in the afternoon I put them in the book as I had promised. Then I cleaned and blacked the grate, laid the fire and dusted out the room, reading as many book titles as I could without slowing my work. Many of Master's books are scientific and I wouldn't make sense of them if I was to open them, but there's two shelves, one of history and one of poetry, that I would dearly like to look into.

When I went back into the kitchen, Mr. Poole was at the sideboard decanting a bottle of port and as I come in he gave me a sharp, critical look which, because of my guilty heart, I could not meet honestly, which shows what comes of sneaking about and, as the saying goes, "trying to serve two masters."

ive days passed and I neither saw nor heard Master. He took all his meals on a tray and the only words he had with any of us came to Mr. Poole who sometimes found orders to chemists tossed on the laboratory stairs which he filled himself, so he was in and out, always in a bad humour. My patience was worn thin on several scores. The weather was bad, rainy and unseasonable cold, so even if I got a few minutes to myself during a day (which mostly I did not get) I spent them standing under the eaves in the court looking out through the rain at the little garden (as it is called, though it is just a green patch with low misshapen bushes at either end) that separates the house from Master's laboratory, and this only made me gloomier still. I'd always fancied that someday I might have a garden of my own, and it is to this end that I am always saving and live so frugal my fellow servants wonder at me, but I know I mun be in service twenty years and be not much closer to this goal than I am now, and here Master has this fair bit of earth. Though, closed in as it is by buildings, the sun has heavy work to get to it, still it seemed to me something could be done with it if anyone had a mind to. But Master is absorbed in his studies and so he crosses and recrosses this bit of garden and never sees there's no need to leave it bare. And here's this big house with six servants in it, all busy enough to be sure, just keeping it in order, keeping all the fires lit and the larder stocked, as if there were a dozen ladies and gentlemen expected any moment, though no one comes much and Master disappears for days at a time, so it's like serving a ghost, who may see what you do or may not.

I brooded on these things when I had the chance and my fellows seemed not much gladder than I. Mr. Poole was like a dog told to wait at the shop door; he was anxious for his master and would jump at every footstep. Poor Annie got a lot of his sharp tongue and bore it, as was her way, silent and drowsy. Cook and I were of the opinion that hard work is the best cure for low spirits, so we made it our project to scrub out the kitchen from top to bottom and even made the narrow windowpanes sparkle. While we was at it, she told me stories of her childhood in the country, for she was a country lass, and how she come into service first working in a grand estate at S_____, as a scullery maid, and what fine hunting parties the ladies and gentlemen had there, and how the mistress was killed falling from her horse and the master closed the whole place up forever and come up to town. That is how Cook come to be in London, which she declares is a vile, filthy place not fit for anyone to live in and she vows she will go back to the country whenever she can.

That was how we passed the days when Master could have been on the moon as across the yard, for all we knew of his doings. Then on the sixth morning Mr. Poole bustled into the kitchen early, looking as cheerful as I imagine he can, and announced that Master would have his breakfast on a tray in his own bedroom and that I was to look sharp and get a fire up in his room as fast as ever I could, for Master was chilled to the bone and the room was that damp he might die of it.

I put my cap on, as it was so early I'd hardly dressed yet, and a clean apron and hurried up to Master's room. I knocked at the door and heard him say, "Come in," but his voice sounded weak and peevish, so I kept my eyes down, giving him a quick curtsy as I went in and made straight for my work. Even though I scarcely looked at him I took in enough to see that he was propped up on his pillows like an invalid looking as pale as death. It didn't take more than a few moments to get the fire up, as I'd laid the grate three days earlier, so I was soon done and stood up to take my leave when Master said, "Mary, let me have a word with you."

I approached him but couldn't look at him as I felt uncomfortable to be spoken to while he was lying in his *bed*, though he seemed to think nothing on it.

"I've read your story," he said, "and I found it most interesting."

"If you did, sir," I said, "then I'm satisfied." I took the chance of speaking to take a quick look at him, but looked away as quick for he had his kind eyes directly on my face.

"Like many a good storyteller," he went on, "you raise more questions in your tale than you answer."

I didn't know what to say to that as it didn't seem a compliment, nor did I understand what questions I could have raised or why he'd call my writing a "tale" as I'd only told what happened, so I said nothing but stood looking at a rose in the carpet like a dumb creature.

"For example," he said, "nowhere do you explain what your relationship to your persecutor was."

And of course I thought, Oh, I never did, and I wondered why I'd left that out, except that I've never liked much to say it even to myself. "I'm sorry for that, sir," I said. "He were my father."

Master drew in his breath and said, "Oh, I suspected as much, but I'm disheartened to hear it."

Again I could think of nothing to say, except perhaps that I'd heard of worse cases than mine, but that seemed out of place somehow, so I said nothing.

"Another thing you never mention, Mary, is how you feel about this monster."

"Oh, I don't think he were a monster, sir," I said. "He were an ordinary man, but drinking did for him as it has for many another."

He was quiet then, and I wondered if I'd said something I shouldn't have. At last he said, "You don't hate this father of yours, Mary?"

"Well, sir, it was like this," I said. "When I come out of hospital, Father was gone and I never seen him since. Marm went to work as a semptress, where she'd a room, and I went out to service ..." I knew I hadn't answered Master's question but he took what I said and seemed to think on it.

"And in your opinion it was only that he drank. You think that drinking caused him to abuse you?" He put this question so careful and serious, as if he really thought I might know the answer and enlighten him, and also it was a question I had thought on considerable myself, especially in the long, dark-filled hours my father put me through as a child, and even afterwards when I was safe from him in the houses of gentlemen like Master, I thought on it, so I tried to give Master my answer as true as ever I could.

"When I was very small," I said, "Father didn't drink so much. He had some little work at the docks, and though he wasn't ever a kind man, he weren't cruel to me. Since his wanting to hurt me came on at the same time as his drinking, I naturally put one as the cause of the other."

"But you're not sure which is the cause of which, Mary?" Master said.

"Many a man drinks sir, and we see some of them only become high-spirited and good-natured, and others as is boisterous or wants a good fight with their fellows. With my father, when he was drinking it was as if he couldn't get enough of seeing suffering, and as I was at hand, it was me he took his pleasure in hurting. He was a different man then—he even looked different, sir, as if the cruel man was always inside him and the drinking brought him out."

"Or *let* him out," Master said softly.

I had not been looking at Master from shyness to say so much, and when he spoke I saw he was fixed on me, attending on my every word, silent and anxious. I felt a terrible strangeness and scarce knew where to look when a knock come on the door and my eyes met Master's in alarm. It was only a moment before the door opened and Mr. Poole come in with Master's breakfast tray, but I saw many things in it: Master's look of sympathy for me, first, and then as I turned to leave I got a full view of Mr. Poole in the cheval glass and saw his look fixed on my back, full of anger, for he could see I had been talking with Master and he couldn't bear it, so I knew, as I hurried out of the room, that I'd best keep to myself as much as I could until that day was out.

*T*hat night Mr. Poole told us Master had made himself ill from too much study and hardly touching his food, so for two days he did not leave his bed. Cook said she knew how to "bring him back," as she put it, by starting him on soup, eggs and weak tea and then gradually bringing him to more solid foods. Mr. Poole insisted that everything must be brought in and done by himself alone, even to laying the fire, though he was good enough to allow me to bring the coals up, a bit of work his narrow shoulders was probably too weak to bear. He said nothing to me about my talk with Master, but he'd his eye upon me at everything I did and if I had a moment's free time he invented some chore to fill it up. I didn't mind him and was glad enough to have my hands filled, as I felt worried about Master and it seemed to me that in doing my part to keep his house running smooth, I might help him to recover his strength.

Cook's method was a good one and in a few days Master was recovered and about his usual routines. One morning as Cook and I was peeling 'tatoes, I spoke to her about the garden, which she called the "yard," because she said it was too run-down to be called a garden. "But that's the waste of it," I said. "Here we go out to the greengrocer for parsley and all herbs when we could easily be growing them here."

"A herb garden," Cook said. "I've thought of it myself. We had one at B⸺ Square, in a yard no bigger than ours here. But the earth would need heavy spading, Mary, and my poor back is too stiff for such work."

"But mine isn't," I said. "Only I've never tried a garden so I wouldn't know how to begin."

"Oh, I could tell you that," Cook said. "I've a green thumb; my mother said it run in our family."

So Cook and I talked on this garden and by the time Mr. Poole come in for tea I'd persuaded her to talk with him on the subject as if it were her own idea, as I knew he'd never agree to it if he thought it come from my head. I went up to my room and amused myself with my writing a bit, then when I come down Cook was smiling at me and said it was all arranged, that Mr. Poole approved of the idea and had given her leave to use any free time we both could find to begin our project. He even told her there was all the tools we would need in the shed off the laboratory and that in Dr. Denman's time there had been a nice bit of garden there and that in his opinion, it were a waste to have it run-down as it was.

So on one thing Mr. Poole and I are agreed.

I was up early the next morning, well before the sun, and I had washed down the front steps on my knees before anyone in the house was awake. This suited me well enough as I never like being looked at as I'm doing this work, especially as so many of the houses near us are now let to all sorts of tradesmen, so there's a constant traffic and not of the nicest gentlemen, either, but those who think it's smart to speak out to a working girl and see if they can distract her from her duties. It was black and foggy out, and the gas lights were still lit so each one had a yellow halo round it and they looked like a line of strange, bright fairy clouds, making eerie dollops of light along the street which was as quiet as death. I did the steps and then all the brass and took my buckets to the curb to empty out. I stood looking at the house front and my first thought was, ours is the finest and best kept on the street. Then, as I was dreaming a little, on how many houses I've been in and how of them all this is the best place I've had, for I'm paid more here, twelve pounds a year, there's a liberal feeling in the kitchen for we all of us eat as well as we could want and haven't even to get our own beer, and though Mr. Poole is hard on me, he's not unfair, and of course our master is a respected gentleman who does many charitable works and as he is a bachelor, there's only him to keep up after and he's as clean in his ways as a military man. As I was musing thus, I saw a lamp go on upstairs in Master's room. I had a misgiving that he might be sleepless or ill, and I gathered up my buckets to go in lest he might ring, but as I did this the lamp went out again.

When I got back to the kitchen I put the big kettles on and got the stove up for Cook, who come in as I was working, surprised to find me there as she is always first up and has the kitchen warm for us and our tea when Annie and I come down. I told her I'd done my morning work and was now free to run out to the markets for her, so we might both have an hour before lunch to start on our garden, and I could see she was very pleased, called me "dear Mary" and said I was the best housemaid she'd ever known and a credit to our house, all of which made me feel pleased with myself and glad I'd come up with our project.

By half after ten everything was done, Cook had the shed key from Mr. Poole and we went out to begin our work. We found the shovels and spades, rakes, a good hoe, gloves, a number of empty pots and even a big bag of soil, all put away neatly in the little shed where, Cook said, they mun have been sitting for twenty years, waiting for hands as would take them up.

I set to work with Cook's direction, and heavy work it was, as the ground was so hard it come up in great clods. Cook said first those ugly bushes mun go and they gave me a fair struggle, though they hardly looked alive, and I thought how all plants do struggle and seem to be longing to flourish no matter how badly they are treated or on what hard, unprofitable soil they fall, so I began to feel a little sad for the poor bushes, but Cook said they'd be the death of our herbs so up they mun come.

We had been at it a good time, me digging and Cook breaking up clods with a spade, when we heard the laboratory door open and Master come out, strolling towards us in a leisurely way and looking so strong and well it was a pleasure to see. Cook got up as he approached and begun dusting herself off, looking very nervous and surprised, as she rarely sees Master, being always in the kitchen, and she said, "Oh, sir, what is the hour? You mun be coming in for your lunch."

So Master come up to us and I gave up shovelling, feeling a little ashamed for I was sweating and dirty and I knew my face must be red from my struggle with the bushes, though I felt proud too, for there they were, got up on the flags and ready to be hauled off. Master said to Cook, "It's only just past eleven. I was going in to write some letters before lunch. You might tell Poole I'll take it in the library and there's certainly no reason to hurry."

Cook bobbed him a curtsy and said, "Very good, sir," and then to me, "I'll be off to get cleaned up and the luncheon on, Mary. You may work a bit longer if you're not tired."

I said I would and Cook hurried off, leaving me leaning on my shovel and Master gazing on me in my dirt. "Well, Mary," he said. "Poole tells me we're to have a garden."

"Yes, sir," I said. "Cook says we may have herbs here and she knows the way of gardening."

"You don't know the way yourself?"

"No, sir," I said. "We had some potted geraniums once, at the Marley School, and that's as close as I've been to growing anything."

Master seemed to light up with interest at my reply. "The Marley School, Mary?" he said. "Why, that is one of my projects."

"Truly, sir? You mean you was a teacher there?"

"No, Mary," he said, seeming to think my idea a funny one. "I've never seen the school. But it was partly my idea and I gave the money for the building and I am on the board still. We see to the running of the school."

I thought it odd that Master would be running a school he never saw, and then I thought if he saw what went on there he might not be looking so pleased, but that made me feel sorry for Master, with his good intentions and his seeming so pleased to find I was a pupil there, so I only said, "It's where I learned to read, sir, so I'm grateful to you."

This delighted Master so his face broke into a smile, as if someone had given him a fine present, and he seemed almost shy to have my thanks for he said, "Well, Mary. So. That's very fine, very gratifying to me. It seems remarkable really, that you should go to my school and end up in my house."

Then I had such a mean thought it left me speechless, for it was this, that considering how rough the school was, it was a wonder I could read and had got as far as I have in the world, which surely even Master mun see isn't very far. So I said nothing, but wiped my sweating forehead on my sleeve and stood looking at Master across the dirt feeling all the world was standing between us and we'd no way ever to cross it, but also that somehow we was also two sides of the same coin, doing our different work in the same house and as close, without speaking, as a dog and his shadow.

Master's smile faded and we looked at each other a moment longer, me feeling no shame at my dirt, but rather proud. Then Master looked down at the shovel pressed in the dirt and said, "Well then, Mary. Good luck with your gardening," and he turned away and went into the house.

So I continued my digging but I felt strange somehow, as if my work would come to no good end and the garden would never be as it was in my imagination, but only a poor stunted, blighted place where nothing would prosper no matter how much Cook and I might try. And I thought of Master who was so kind and thoughtful today, not distant as he used to seem before we had our talk and he read my history, and I remembered the question he had asked as to whether I hated my father for his ill use of me and how I had failed to answer it and Master had not pressed me, for he must have seen what I now understood, that I hadn't answered because I don't know the answer.

I believe to hate my father would be to give in and make small my real feeling which is strong but not like hate, as that seems simple, pure and clean. Yet I feel that my father put this dark place in me that brings sadness on me unawares, when I should be happy to have my good place and such friends as I have and someone like Cook who can advise me on the way of gardening, and who is simple herself and finds happiness in doing her work and knowing her place. But for me, though I can get past it, there's often this darkness and sadness, unexpected and coming from things that should bring happiness, like the thought of the garden and the working in it with Cook, but then it rises up inside like a blackness and I really am in that blackness where my father left me, with no way out and nothing to do but wait until somehow there's some merciful release and I come to myself again.

So I feel my father made me thus, or left me thus, with this sadness which has been hard to bear and will likely never leave me no matter what fortune I have, and it sets me apart from my fellows who seem never to know it. While I can't forgive my father, neither can I regret what I am, and there are times when I would not give up the sadness and darkness because it do seem to me true that this is part of how we mun see life if we are to say we saw it, and it has to do with our being alone and dying alone, which we all mun do. So it seems to me that many people, especially gentlefolks, spend a great deal of money and all their time trying to push all sadness from their lives, which in my view they can never do, because it is *there*, no matter how well off we may be in this world, and it just mun be got through. I see I have this patience to wait it out, and the truth is no matter how dark I feel I would never take my own life, because when the darkness is over, then what a blessing is the feeblest ray of light!

And this is truly something I see in Master and why I am so drawn to serve him and what I think he mun see in me, and why he has wanted to look into my history, because we are both souls who knew this sadness and darkness inside and we have both of us learned to wait.

I couldn't seem to come back to myself after my talk with Master over the garden. It was as if I had been digging up my own childhood and for the rest of the day my thoughts was as hard and black as the soil. These many years I've seldom really thought on my past and have tried to put it behind me, going on with my work, for I see no good in brooding on things that can never be changed. I know Cook thought it odd to see me downcast at lunch, as she was pleased with me and full of plans for our garden, but I could scarcely lift my head. Afterwards I took my buckets and brushes and went out to scrub the flags in the front hall. This is a long, slow, dirty job which I like to do on my knees with my skirts tied up, using a lot of water and brushes, first to loosen up all the dirt, then a deal more until it is clear again, taking it up with my big sponges and pouring more out until I've fair made a little river of the hall. Before I started I got the fireplace going so the hall would dry out fast when I was done, but as I worked it made me so hot that I was dripping and felt I was in a steam cabinet such as I have read about in the bathing establishments. I worked and worked, scrubbing hard, sloshing through the filthy water to fill my buckets, going round the house and in through the area, so many passersby saw me hurrying along in my bare feet and skirts tied up, then I had to use half a bucket on my feet at the front step before going back in. I was waiting for my spirits to lift with the dirt, but they would not. Then I had a thought that struck me so hard I dropped my brush and rose up on my knees like a rabbit trying to hear the fox and that was this, that my father is still alive somewhere.

Why this should so stun me I don't know, but it did, and all at once it was as if he was not just alive somewhere, but in the very hall with me. Our big house was silent all around me. Master had gone to his laboratory after lunch and Mr. Poole was out at the chemist's for him. Mr. Bradshaw had his day off, Cook and Annie was in the kitchen, so I knew there was no one about, yet I seemed to hear someone walking towards me.

I glanced back at the fire, for a chill had come over me, and gave myself a shake as if I could shake off the dread. But it would not go away and I felt as I used to feel when I heard his bootstep in the alley, that I could pick out his step from among a thousand, for it was always coming for me and each step fairly called my name. Then I felt the water running down my face was changed, that it was tears. I could not think when was the last time I found myself crying. "Oh lord," I said out loud. "What's becoming of me?"

So I had to force myself back to my work and just let the tears run with all the other water I had about me, which they did and quite freely. I thought on Master and how his notice of me has stirred up all this confusion, sadness and dread, all feelings I thought I had put to rest, and how it is doing me no good at all, yet I think I cannot undo what's been done, nor should I try.

At dinner Mr. Poole was in a fuss because Master was closed up in his laboratory again and he'd said just to leave him a little cold mutton on the cabinet stairs as he was on no account to be disturbed. So, Mr. Poole said, he feared Master had so little regard for his own health it was getting to be all the staff could do to keep him well. I felt too low to say much, not that I'm ever talkative, especially when Mr. Poole is about, and Cook noticed I wasn't eating. "Mary," she said, "you'd best be to bed straight away. I fear rising so early and working so hard has knocked you up and we can't do without you." Mr. Poole raised his eyebrows at this and gave me a long look. Then he said, "You do look pale, Mary. I believe Mrs. Kent is right."

I thought I would fall over to hear a kind word from Mr. Poole and I know my mouth dropped open, but then I thought I must be looking near dead and perhaps they was right and I was coming down with something. So I said, "Yes, sir," and Cook told me to drink all my beer and be off, which I did, getting in bed by eight, even before Annie. I fell straight to sleep, nor did I hear Annie get in, and I think I didn't even move until near dawn when my eyes flew open like windows and my heart was pounding because I knew something was amiss in our house.

Someone was climbing up the back steps, not to our attic but below that, between the kitchen and Master's bedroom. The house was that quiet and still, I could hear the floorboards creak like thunder. I heard a step, then another, then silence. My palms were wet and my legs felt so weak, I thought perhaps I'd been dreaming and somehow carried it over into waking, and as I heard nothing else, I made myself calm by breathing in and out very slow.

Then I heard another step, halting-like, then nothing. "Now I am awake," I said out loud, hoping Annie might be awake too, but she didn't move and as my eyes were used to the dark I could see her face, slack with sleep, and I had a funny thought, that Annie is like a dog at the end of a hunt when she sleeps and if you put a plate of food under her nose no doubt but she would dream she was eating.

Another step, my thought went away, then another. He was on the landing now and moving towards Master's room.

I thought, of course, it *mun* be Master coming in from his work and moving quietly so as not to disturb Mr. Bradshaw who has his room under those stairs. And I felt foolish for my terror, though, I thought, this is the second time today I have heard footsteps. I heard the door to Master's room open and he went in, so of course it was him, though there was something in the step, so halting, as if he was dragging one foot a little, whereas Master has a light, even way of walking.

But he's tired, I thought, and anyhow it's probably my fancy, as how could I make that out listening through two floors? Then I remembered that my father had that halting way about his walk and how I used to hear my own name in it, long on the first part—Maare, and then short -ry, Maare-ry, until I thought I would scream.

And it come back to me again, as it did so hard this afternoon, that my father is alive still, even if it is only in my own poor head, that he was gone for a while and that somehow Master's kindness and interest has brought him back to life for me.

BOOK 2

*W*hat comes before brings me to last
night and so I begin this new book which I bought at
Lett's this morning, paying sevenpence for the purpose
of recording my life in this house.

This morning Mr. Poole and Mr. Bradshaw were
debating on the best means to move the cheval glass

from Master's bedroom to the cabinet in the laboratory, for it seemed Master had called Mr. Poole in early to request that this be done. Mr. Poole was for wrapping it up entire in blankets and rope and calling in the knife boy to help, as it is a big, heavy glass and will need considerable care. Mr. Bradshaw, who is handy with tools, was of the opinion that the glass should be taken from the frame, on which it is hung by a swivelling joint, carried to the laboratory in the two pieces and put back together there. While they discussed the best method, I found myself puzzling on why Master would want a looking glass in his laboratory, but I didn't venture a guess as I knew Mr. Poole would be annoyed to have any of Master's wishes questioned and would tell me to mind my own concerns. They were having such a disagreement, though they spoke to one another most respectfully, it was clear Mr. Bradshaw thought Mr. Poole an unbending, tiresome old crank and Mr. Poole thought Mr. Bradshaw a brash upstart, and both were worried about the job for fear something would happen to the mirror and which one would get the blame if his method failed, that I was fair amused. I knew Mr. Poole was beside himself when he told me to take up Master's breakfast tray to the drawing room and see what his plans for luncheon was. I set up the tray and Cook gave me a pretty vase with a single rose in it to put on the side, which she'd saved from a bunch bought at market yesterday, so it made a lovely touch on the tray, I thought. Cook asked if I felt better and I said I did, as I'd gone to bed so early and slept well. I carried the tray up through the house and it seemed my poor spirits had truly lifted. It was a bright day out for a change and the sunlight streamed through the panes so it pleased me to see how clear they was, and how all the cabinets and tables gleamed with the polishing I'd given them. When I knocked at the drawing room Master called out, "Come in," sounding cheerful I thought, and so he was, for when I opened the door he looked up from the desk where he was writing and said, "Ah, Mary. You've brought my breakfast. I hope it's a big one."

"I believe it is, sir," I said, bringing the tray to him. He cleared his papers out of the way so I could set it down before him. "Cook said you ate nothing on your plate last night that would keep a mouse alive so she mun stuff you when she can."

"Last night I couldn't eat, Mary," he said, diving into the rashers before I had the plate square before him. "I've been at an impasse in my work for some time now, but last night"—he paused to bite into his toast—"last night all the barriers fell before me." He chewed a moment, looking like a half-starved child, I thought. "Excellent toast," he finished.

"I'd say rather it were this morning, sir," I said. "For I heard you coming in with the sun. You can't have had three hours' sleep."

"I don't feel tired at all," he said.

"Perhaps you've found a way to go on without sleep, sir," I said. "But sooner or later it mun catch up with you and you'll make yourself ill again."

Master chewed for a moment without speaking and

as I was standing behind him I couldn't see his face. "Are you chiding me, Mary?" he asked.

There was something in his tone that wasn't pleased and I felt so taken aback by it that I didn't speak, but stood there staring at his back until he turned in his chair and looked me up and down, his face set in that expression of kindly interest that always touches me to say what is in my heart, and he began to speak to me softly saying, "Am I too much trouble for you, Mary? Do you wish you had a more regular master who went out to the courts every day, or perhaps to a bank, and always had dinner at the same time, unless, of course, he was dining at his club?"

As he spoke I was shaking my head, and when he paused I jumped in saying, "Oh no, sir. I never wish to serve anyone but you."

"Of course that is what you must say, Mary. But you're very young, and very fair, as I'm sure you know. How can you be expected to find any reward in giving up your youth to serve a life as old and dry and dull as mine?"

His words stung me and I found my tongue. "And what should I do other, sir?" I said. "Should I like a house full of fashionable ladies, fetching toys and shoes for disagreeable children, scrubbing floors and carrying up coal for gentlefolk who never look at me except to see if I've not done summat amiss? No, sir, thank you. I'd a bit of that before I come here."

Master smiled at my outburst. "You do put things strongly, Mary."

"I'm sorry, sir," I said. "I speak out because I can't bear for you to think I'm wishing for some other life than the one I have. If I chide you, it's only that I worry for your health—we do all of us, when you close yourself up and do without food or sleep for days on end."

"I suppose I have a master too," he said. "And mine, Mary, if you can conceive it, is more demanding than yours."

For a moment I was puzzled to understand what he meant, but then I saw that he was speaking of his work, his "scientific investigations," as Mr. Poole calls them, which cannot be interrupted, and I remembered he said that he'd broken through all the barriers last night. "Won't your 'master' give you a little rest now, sir?" I said. "After last night?"

Master looked startled, as if he'd forgotten I was there and suddenly found me too close by, too sudden. He looked at me hard until I felt he was trying to solve the question of how I'd got to be standing before him, having said what I'd just said, and as I didn't know the answer myself, I didn't speak. At last he said, "Do you truly never wish for another life, Mary?"

"No, sir," I said. "What would be the good of that?"

"Oh," he replied. "So it is only that you believe you cannot have one."

"Not only that, sir," I said. "Though I suppose that's part of it."

"And if you could. If I told you there was a way to have a life in which you could act only as *you* please, *when* you please, with no consequences, no regrets, then wouldn't you say yes?"

Master fair toppled over his chair as he said this, and seemed so intent on my answer that I felt I had better think hard and give it true as I could. But I couldn't understand really what he meant, except that I might dream of a life out of service, that I might want to be a lady, who has nothing to do but amuse herself. I've seen plenty of these and never envied them one moment, as it does seem their lives are full of mean spirit, if they are full of anything, because they are so idle. So I started to say no, I wouldn't want such a life, but then it seemed Master was so vexed over the thought of there being no consequences that he must not mean what I thought, so I only said, "I don't believe that there is any actions without consequences."

Master looked surprised—disappointed, I thought. He seemed to remember that I was only a housemaid— I could see that in his face and it hurt my pride, though why I should feel so I can't say, as I'm proud to be what I am and had only just told him as much. He said, "Of course that's true, Mary. Under *normal* circumstances what you say is quite true," and he said the word "normal" as if it was the space between us, and mayhap he is right about that. I felt I'd failed to imagine the world Master must be in always, where many things is possible because of his being a man of science. This cast me down considerable. Master turned back to his breakfast and I had to clear my throat to get his attention and ask what his plans was for luncheon.

"Tell Poole I'll take it in the library, Mary," he said. "And that my solicitor will be joining me for dinner at the regular hour."

"Very good, sir," I said, as I've heard Mr. Poole say when Master gives his wishes. It seemed to strike Master as funny to hear me say it, for he turned a little in my direction and said, "Where is our Mr. Poole this morning, Mary, that you are sent on the breakfast mission?"

"He and Mr. Bradshaw is struggling with your cheval glass, sir," I said. "They aren't in agreement as to how it should be transported." This made Master smile in his easy way and I felt we was back on our good footing.

"Will they succeed, in your opinion, Mary?"

"Oh yes, sir," I said. "I've no doubt on it. But it will take time. It seems there's a strategy to it."

"Well, I wish them luck, Mary," he said, "and I think I'll avoid the scene of the struggle."

"Yes, sir," I said, turning to leave. I was nearly at the door when Master added, "Don't worry about me too much, Mary. I'll take better care of myself now. I promise you that."

The rest of the day passed quietly. Mr. Bradshaw and Mr. Poole got the mirror down the stairs and out into the backyard without anything going amiss. I was at hanging up the drawing-room curtains, which I had washed in the morning, feeling I should take advantage of the sunshine to get something dried out, as we've had so little sun of late, and Mr. Poole called to me to come and get the laboratory key from his pocket and open the door for him as he couldn't do it himself, being under the weight of the mirror, which they'd wrapped up all in one piece, so Mr. Poole had won out. I left the curtains in the basket, ran to his side and dug out the key from his pocket. I squeezed in before them as they was huddled under the overhang like dogs in the rain, and shoved the big door open before them. Then, as I couldn't get back around them, there was nothing to do but step inside. I felt a thrill, though I dared not show it, that I was seeing at last where Master spends so much of his time. It seemed my eyes couldn't take it all in quick enough, though truly there was not that much to see.

The first room is the old "theatre" where Dr. Denman used to perform operations for students. Master hasn't bothered to change it, so there is an evil-looking table bolted to the floor in the centre and around the room two rows of benches on raised steps, each with a ledge in front of it, so I pictured the students leaning forward on their elbows to see someone being cut open, for Dr. Denman was a surgeon, Mr. Poole says, and he had a great reputation among students, though they sometimes called him "the butcher," because they said he would find a reason to cut open a perfect well man out of his desire to have a look inside him.

The room is quite large and the windows is all at the top and even on the ceiling, so that the light comes in great streaks that cross over one another, making pools in some spots and leaving others in darkness.

Master doesn't use the room for much but storing things. There were boxes stacked around, some with straw pouring out and also piles of the straw in corners. There's tools scattered around too, most carelessly. I saw a hammer on the floor alongside one of the boxes, and some sort of prying tool, and an axe half buried in straw. Spiders has made themselves comfortable it looked for a long time to me, especially up in the corners and in the windows where I think they must like to be to catch such foolish flies and bugs as is drawn to light. The floor was of smooth flags that I could make shine as ours in the hall do, if I'd a week or so with no other project, such was the grime that covered them. On the far end of the room was a staircase leading up to a landing and a second door covered with dark red baize which looked as it might open into a heart, and it was to this door that Mr. Poole, Mr. Bradshaw and the knife boy was struggling with the big mirror. I saw they meant to haul it up and Mr. Poole called out to me to take up the key as was hanging on the wall next to the door. I thought it odd to lock a door, then put the key next to it, but this is Master's habit when he wants Mr. Poole to enter the cabinet, as there is only one key which Master does usually keep upon himself. Mr. Poole bid me open the door so I squeezed by them on the steps and did so.

The theatre had made me feel sad. To see a room no one cares for is to me like seeing a child or an animal that mun struggle without love, or perhaps it is because the rooms of those who don't care for life—or for anyone in it—are so often neglected. So this room gave me a start, for this was a room Master loved, but there was something else I cannot name, some deep sadness, of one, I thought, who is not loved. Everything was neat, as is Master's way, and I saw he don't need any help to keep it so. There was a fireplace with a good chair drawn up to it and a tea table beside that. The fireplace had a fine brass fender on it with two beautiful brass babies on either side, lying back a bit as if to warm their feet, such bright smiles and a happy manner about them as lifted my heart to look at them and think of who might have been amused to make such pretty things. They are finer than any of the fenders we have in the house, and, of course, in want of a polishing, though there was no dust on them, so Master, or Mr. Poole, must rub them with a cloth. There was a good carpet on the floor and shelves lined with books. A big old blackened kettle on the hearth, such as is used in the country, and tea things, very fine, with a rose and a pansy in the pattern. This was one end of the room, a proper study and retreat for any gentleman. The far end was a different picture. There were three long windows with a ledge before each, wide enough to sit upon and looking out into the court, I imagined, and they let in the light, and a deal of it there was, pouring over the long table set before them, and over the three big presses filled with drawers, each labelled in Master's fine hand. The carpet ended well before, so the table stood on the cold flags. On the table was all manner of strange bottles and containers, long glass tubes with cork stoppers leading from one to another, and such tools as funnels, odd-shaped spoons, measures and scales, screens —so many and different kinds that I could scarce take them in—and though everything was orderly, there was so much I had a feeling of confusion. Mr. Poole and Mr. Bradshaw had sent the knife boy off and was unwrapping the glass in the corner; they'd put it down in the end of the room that was like a sitting room, which I thought was right as it seemed such a fine old piece would look like an orphan child in this cold part of the room, and I wondered if they chose the spot out of the same sense I had, or if it was Master's wish to keep these two worlds forever apart. I stepped back onto the carpet, feeling as I did so fair in retreat, and I stood looking back at the table which I understood was where Master did his science and I had this thought, that here was the place that was killing him and I hated it. I set my heart against it.

Then Mr. Poole called my name impatiently, saying I might go back to my work, and I turned to see myself looking at my own reflection in the glass, for they had it all unwrapped and in place, and as I peered at my own figure for a moment it seemed I was looking back at myself from the edge of the world, and if I didn't step carefully I would fall off into nothing. I shook myself, for I seemed to be standing in a dream, and took myself back to my work, but though I was busy the rest of the day I felt such ill-content as makes every move a chore.

Oh, why is my heart so heavy?

I know it is that Master called me fair, and has

stirred up my vanity to be something I am not. Before I sat down to write I lit the candle and looked at my face in the glass for a long time. As I put on my shift I stopped a moment to look at my body. How white my skin looks in the candlelight. I brushed my hair down and let it fall over my breasts and I thought, is this a sight my master would care to see?

Ten days has passed with us all so busy I haven't had the time to put down a word. Master is with us and in high spirits. He goes in and out and has had company three nights in five, including a dinner party for eight what had Cook and me run off our feet two days in preparation. He has not gone to his laboratory once and seems not to think of it. When I said to Mr. Poole that the dinner talk mun be very scientific, all the gentlemen being learned doctors (except Mr. Utterson who mun have what I've heard called a legal mind and so adds in his views as they might be useful), he laughed at me and said, "Why, Mary, the talk is all of a show Mr. Littleton has seen, in which a young lady flies over the audience on a trapeze, hanging upside down by her knees and even by her ankles, dressed in a bit of a suit covered with silver stars that shows off her figure completely and leaves naught to be imagined about her."

This shocked me and I said, "Surely Master has not been to such a spectacle." Mr. Poole gave me one of his long, dry looks which may of meant, "Of course he has," or "How could you think of it?" I've no idea which.

Master has been drinking and eating more than usual as well, which I think cannot be bad for him. He has a fondness for good wine and Cook says our cellar is as good as can be found in London. These days Master has been sending Mr. Poole into it regular to fetch some bottle as has achieved "a perfection" so Cook calls it, and Mr. Poole says it is a wonder how Master knows just what is down there and how long it's been and even exactly where it is. These he serves to his visitors, being a most generous host who shares the best he has, and afterwards when they are gone he may take the opened bottle into the library and finish it off over a book, or just sitting quiet before the fire. There I found him last night after dinner when Mr. Poole sent me to get up the fire, as it was dying and the house has a chill in it of late, though it is fair summer, that we cannot seem to drive out with coal or cleaning.

Master was standing close to the fire, as is his way, and only turned to say "Come in" to my knock. "I've come to see to your fire, sir," I said and he nodded, stepping back, but only a little, as if he couldn't bear to be separated from the bit of heat that was left, and he said, "Good, Mary. I believe it is nearly gone and I'm feeling so restless I don't think I'll attempt sleep for a while." So I had to kneel down at his feet, which made me uncomfortable, and go about gathering up what ash was left and laying in a new store of coals.

"You must be chilled yourself, Mary," Master said. "Our kitchen is such a vast, dark cave of a place."

"No, sir," I said. "Cook has had the big oven up all day, so it's like a furnace to me. I don't mind the cold anyway, for I'm used to it." As I spoke the coal was taking and a swell of heat seemed to pour out from under my hands, so I fell back on my knees while the wave rose up before me.

"There," Master said, drawing close and holding his hands out before him. "Good. I can never get used to the cold, I'm afraid."

I stood up and backed away, wiping my black hands on my apron, so that Master could go back to his fire-gazing, and I said, "That's because you're a gentleman sir, and have thinner blood than mine, no doubt."

Master gave a little laugh and spoke to me without looking at me. "As a doctor and a scientist Mary, I feel it is my obligation to tell you that your theory has no basis in fact."

"I beg your pardon, sir," I said, meaning I was sorry to have spoken foolishness, but Master thought I had not understood him so he turned to me and said, "All human blood is the same, Mary. Under the microscope I could tell your blood from a monkey's, perhaps, but not from my own."

"I see, sir," I said. I felt a little annoyed to be lectured on my stupidity, so I looked right at Master and to my surprise he seemed to blush, though perhaps it was only that the fire had made his blood rise, which I felt timid to observe in my own head as it might be another mistake on my part. Master took up the decanter from the tray Mr. Poole had brought in and poured himself out a glass of port while I stood watching, not able to think what to say next. Looking on me seemed to soften his thoughts for he asked pleasantly, "How does your gardening progress, Mary? I haven't looked at it in weeks, it seems, I've been so preoccupied with projects."

"Hardly have I, sir," I said. "But it do seem that as soon as some seed we planted comes up, two such as we don't want are on each side vying for the sun."

"Weeds, Mary," Master replied, setting his glass down hard on the tray as if to crush out the weeds growing there. "Where do they come from if you haven't somehow put them there?"

"Why, the air must be full of them, sir," I said. "For they are so much about that we see whole forests as is grown up without cultivation. But what strikes me is why, once they find a bit of soil, are weeds so much stronger than the things we want to grow?"

"And do you have an answer to that question, Mary?" he asked.

"I have thought on it, sir," I said. "And it seems, being wild, they have a greater will to life."

Master gave me a ghastly smile and repeated what I'd said as if it was some profound truth he'd just received from an opening in the sky.

"I think it's true of many things as is deprived, and

children too," I said, "that they grow strong when no one cares for them and seem to love whatever life they can eke out and will kill to keep it, while the pampered child sickens and dies."

Master poured out another glass of port and I saw his hand was shaking. His face was pale and drops of moisture had formed on his upper lip and forehead, so he looked like a man having a fright instead of talking with his housemaid on the subject of weeds. He brought the glass to his lips abruptly, seeming not to taste the little bit he swallowed and gazing at me over the glass with lowered eyelids as if he couldn't believe what his eyes showed him and so sought another line of vision.

"Sir," I said, "are you well?"

"Why do you strike me so, Mary?" he replied, sounding hoarse.

"I beg your pardon, sir?" I said.

"The things you say and that earnest, sober manner you have, as if you always mean more than you say."

I looked down as he spoke, feeling I couldn't ever look up again, and so confused my mouth went dry. Master stood just so without moving, his glass in the air.

"I'm sorry for it, sir," I said. "If I seem forward. I only want to be honest and answer you always as best I can."

Still Master said nothing and while I stood waiting we heard the sound of raindrops against the window, very soft and seeming far off, so that the room, with the flickering fire and drawn curtains, was a haven from the cold darkness outside.

"How many people know about you, Mary?" he said at last. "How many know how you came by those scars on your hands?"

I drew my hands away, so surprised was I to hear Master speak of them. "Only you, sir," I said. "It is not a story I care to tell." I wanted to add that no one had cared to know, which struck me as the wonder of it, but Master cut in quickly.

"I thought you could not tell it," he said. "It was for that I asked you to write it down."

"Yes, sir," I said. "You was right in that."

"Can I trust you, Mary?" he asked. "As you have trusted me?"

Then I thought Master must be planning to give me a piece of writing on his own life, which did strike me as too fanciful, especially as he seemed so uncertain and anxious about asking me. "I hope you can, sir," I said, "in all things."

He put down his glass and peered at me another moment, so that I thought he was trying to read my character. "Yes," he said. "I think I can." Then he went to his writing desk and took out an envelope, which he tapped against his palm as if still weighing whether to give it me or not. "You have a half-day this week, don't you, Mary?" he asked, still looking at the letter.

"I do, sir," I said. "On Thursday."

"I want you to deliver this letter for me," he said.

"It must go by hand on that day. And no one must know of it—not Mr. Poole, not Annie, you understand."

"I do, sir," I said. He held the letter out to me but I felt too timid to step forward and take it, though I was that curious to read the address I could not take my eyes from it. So we stood there a moment, very awkward, then Master closed the distance to me and I put my hand out not thinking, except as I might to stop him. When he stepped back the letter was in my hand.

Master watched me closely as I turned it over and read the address. I struggled to keep my face from showing what I felt, for I knew exactly where it was and I wondered how Master even knew of such a street. No gentleman could have any business at that address as could do anything but bring ruin to his name. That it was addressed to a Mrs. Farraday troubled me further. How could Master know of a *woman* who would live in such a place as I knew this to be?

"Can you deliver it, Mary?" Master said softly.

I turned the letter over again so I would not have to look at it, then, feeling it was burning my fingers to hold it, I opened my wrist buttons and slipped it up my sleeve. "Yes, sir," I said. "I can certainly do it."

"There will be no reply, other than a yes or no. This you can give to me on Friday, when you have returned."

"Yes, sir," I said.

"It's a matter of some importance to me," Master said. "I must be able to count absolutely on your integrity . . . and Mary," he paused until I looked up and met his steady, calm gaze, "on your silence."

"Please, sir," was all I could say.

"Then I am confident," he replied, "and now I put the business from my mind." With that he turned back to the fire while I stood a moment looking at his back, at his hair which is thick, silver and a little long for the fashion, curling over his collar, and I thought I would like to cut a lock of it. Then, shocked at my own strange whims, which it seems I never can control, I went out, closing the door quietly behind me.

*I*t is very late and our house is asleep, but I cannot sleep. I lay beside Annie for hours, staring into the darkness, having such thoughts as leave me bitter and confused. I got up at last and lit the candle to sort things out if I can by putting them down. The moon is full tonight and makes a white, chilly light all along the windowsill where I sit. There's no view but the back of the house next ours and a small space filled with blackness and stars.

It's all very well for Master to say he can now put the matter out of his mind, and doubtless he has done so while I am left sleepless, feeling not trusted and valued as I should, but anxious and afraid. The letter lies hidden in my dresser, folded inside my other night shift, and there it must stay for another night before I can set myself to the unhappy task of delivering it.

After I left Master last night I told myself this only pertains to some charitable work, such as is often his pleasure to do, and I will see as soon as I come to the house that it is the beacon of honest light in the darkness of poverty and filth that lies all round it. In fact I know there *is* a house on that square run in part by the church (churches as must lock their doors of an evening, such is the character of those parishioners), a house that is for homeless children where they can rest a night or two until some place can be found for them. But I know well enough that this street runs onto the square but don't face it, so it cannot be the same place. And even if it were, why would Master have such a need for secrecy? In general he is pleased enough to have it known abroad that he is one who cares for those less fortunate.

No, everything about this letter is not what it should be, and I dread the morning I must go out and see to its delivery. Yet I do feel Master would not call upon me in such a way if it were not, as he put it, of some importance to him—of some very considerable importance, I should say—and I know also that he must set a great deal of trust in my character and the goodwill I bear him, to choose me over Mr. Poole to carry out this request.

For surely Master knows no one could be more devoted to him than Mr. Poole. So there can only be one reason and that is this is some business he don't want Mr. Poole to know of, which do lead again to the feeling that this is something no respectable gentleman mun engage upon.

How my heart misgives me, to be singled out, because of what Master knows about me, as the one most likely to keep whatever painful secret this is.

*S*o this miserable errand is finished and I hope I may never go on another such. I felt, returning finally to my own small room at the top of this fine house, that I was coming into the fresh light of day after a trip through Hades.

I was up early and did my work in the morning and hurriedly, as I always do on my half-day so I won't be behind the next day. I got in a great lot of coal, did all the dusting, stripped down Master's bed and turned the mattress, swept out the carpet with tea leaves, then made up the room again, the drawing room dusted and the fender polished. I got two buckets of water and washed me in the kitchen near the stove, which I usually enjoy, and Cook sat by talking to me. But she would ask what my plan was for my day and I lied, saying I was to stop to cheapen some cloth for a new cloak, as my woollen is too warm for this time of year, and that I would go to Regent's Park as I always do, rain or shine, on my half-day, to see the roses and chat with the gardener there, a fine old country fellow named Mr. Tott, who always looks out for me when I go there and talks to me about the roses. My heart smote me to be lying to Cook, and thinking on where I was bound made me feel so low I could scarcely bring it off, but Cook seemed satisfied enough and wished me a good afternoon. Then I got dressed as I always do, in my good crinoline, print frock, bonnet and gloves, thinking as I put on my cloak that it was a waste to be going out in such attire, what usually makes me feel so festive and cheerful, on an errand that seemed fair to breaking my heart. I had the letter slipped in my cloak pocket that morning, so out I went wishing for all the world that it was a bit of cloth and a walk in the park I was bound for.

I took the omnibus to St. James's Park so that I could have part of my walk coming and going through some quiet green place and so settle my resolution going in and lift my spirits coming out. The weather was grey and drizzly but not cool, and in spite of it many people were strolling about, taking such fresh air as they could find. From there I had a long walk, through thick crowds of people of all sorts out to do their shopping, and carriages surging by with the drivers shouting at anyone foolish enough to try to cross a road, the horses all in a lather, wild-eyed, unable to look right nor left for their blinkers but driven forward by the whip and the mad sound of hooves everywhere, always a sad and frightening sight to me, so I clung to the buildings, moving along slowly and being bumped by those coming in and out of the stalls. Then, as if there was some signpost or boundary, all the noise and commerce gave out, the streets narrowed and the whole scene grew dark and mean—low doorways, lampless and dirty, many standing open and the unlucky residents lounging about on the steps or simply in the dirt itself. There were children everywhere, crouching in the doorways, collected in groups on every corner, working their ways singly or in a pair, through the grown people on the sidewalk with an eye always to pockets that might be liberal or just untended—cunning, sharp-faced, pale, starving, vicious children such as have neither homes to return to nor anyone who might care whether they are ever seen or heard from again. On one corner I passed a solemn girl sweeping the crossing and crying out in a sweet, sad voice for a penny. I dug down in my cloak pocket and came up with one, which, when we had reached the other side, I pressed into her outstretched hand. She barely glanced at me but closed her white fingers tight around the coin—the first she'd seen all day, I had no doubt—and turned back to her crossing, calling out to a loutish man who brushed past me roughly in his hurry to be about whatever bad business he had in mind. I stopped to look back at the child and saw myself in her hopeful, sad little face—only I was more fortunate than she, because Marm made such a home for me as she could and did not turn me into the streets. I had no brothers and sisters who must be fed too, and when I had the good luck to go to school, I found the strength to wrest a little learning from my poor teachers, who was starving nearly as bad as we was.

These streets were not the ones I ran down as a child, though they might be and will be near enough to them soon, as the poor buildings give out under the burden of so many. Even as a child it seemed to me that what made such places wicked was not so much that they was dirty, crowded, ugly and falling down, but that the people who come to live in them know this is a place where no rules or manners need ever be applied and so they act exactly as they feel. Were the gentle classes put into such a place and bidden to live there, they would not know how to act.

I kept my eyes down and hurried along, feeling I was moved only by a dull tug of sadness coming out of my own childhood but now attached to this errand, which I could not think upon without a shudder. Again I told myself that doubtless this was some good thing Master had contrived, to lighten the suffering around me with a little food, a bed, or a book, but though I advised myself, I could not believe it. Here and there were housefronts of a better stamp than their neighbours— not clean by any means, nor inviting, but not in such a state of disrepair, not betraying every sign of want and despair, and at length I found myself standing before one such which bore the same number as Master had written on the letter.

There was a step to separate this doorway from the filth of the street and I lifted my skirts to perch upon it. I found no knocker nor any sign of a bell, so I pounded the wood a few times hard with my fist, waited, hearing nothing, then pounded again. This time I heard the sound of someone moving, a rustling of skirts and a quick step. In a moment the door flew open and I was seized up by the cold, mean, hungry eyes of a woman who I could see greeted every new face as an occasion for suspicion and contempt. She was tall, not well dressed but not in the poor rags of her neighbours on the street by any means, and her hair, which was wiry, silver with age, untidy, seemed to stand out about her face in anger. Though her dress was clean it was cut too low for morning, and the bones that protruded at her throat, where some gentlewoman might place a locket on a bit of ribbon, stuck out looking raw, angry, like the rest of her. When she spoke, which she did at once, her voice was husky, her accent as rude as if she hated the words she spoke.

"Well, here's a fine young miss at my doorstep," she said. "Having been turned out of her position, if I don't miss my guess, for pinching the silver, or was it the brandy, my girl."

"I'm looking for Mrs. Farraday," I said.

"And you're looking *at* her, too," was her response.

I drew the letter from my sleeve, my fingers trembling so it was all I could do to unfasten the buttons, and as I did I explained myself, wanting only for this business to be concluded and myself far away. "I've a letter from Dr. Jekyll," I said. "He has bidden me deliver it to you and wait on your answer, which you may give me direct without writing," and I pulled the letter out. Before I could hand it to her she had snatched it from my fingers, breaking the seal eagerly. "Harry Jekyll," she said, "and what does he want with Mrs. Farraday today?" She withdrew the page from the envelope, extracting two bank notes and slipping them into the front of her dress so quick and nimble I couldn't make out their amounts, then stood perusing the letter with her eyebrows raised and a self-satisfied smirk on her lips. It shocked me to hear Master referred to so familiar, and I had such a feeling of revulsion for her that I drew back a little on my step and tried to occupy my thoughts with the wonder of such a woman being able to read.

"I thought it would come to something like this," she said at length, looking me up and down as if she thought I must be an accomplice.

"I'm afraid I know nothing of it," I said.

"Count yourself lucky, then, my girl," she replied. "I wish I knew nothing of such a one as is here sent to me."

I was silent and she continued her perusal of the letter, hissing over it like some snake who has come upon a mouse, and darting quick, glittering looks at me over the top of the page. "These terms is acceptable," she said. "I'll say that for Harry Jekyll, he knows the price o' things."

"Then your answer is yes," was all I said.

She folded up the paper, stuffed it back in the envelope and sent it to lie with the bank notes in her bosom, all the while smiling at me in such a hateful, confident way as made me shrink inside my clothes. I had a dread that she was about to touch me.

"Oh, you look innocent enough," she said. "And you're very cool, aren't you. Proud too, I'll wager, but time will take care of that."

I said nothing, but I met her insulting eyes with my own and poured out through them such feelings as seemed fairly to sober her, for she lost interest in baiting me and said, "Tell your master it will take me a week to clear everyone out. I can't turn out such as have already paid. Then another week to make the"—she paused over the word—"alterations he wants."

"Very well," I said, feeling so mystified at her response that I stood a moment turning it over in my mind. "I'll tell him your answer is yes, in two weeks' time."

"You may tell him whatever you want," she said. "And give him Mrs. Farraday's compliments for choosing such a milk-faced, lying little la-di-dah for a messenger, and tell him next time he has business with me, he'd best come on it himself. I think he's not above it," and with that she closed the door hard in my face, leaving me feeling a gush of relief, for I thought now that was over and I might spend the rest of my life without standing again in such a doorway with such a woman. I turned away and hurried down the busy street, looking neither right nor left but straight ahead, only wanting to be home in my quiet room where I might best mull over what could possibly be the meaning of this unhappy business.

his morning I was up early—indeed I slept poorly all night, doubtless from the weight of guilt I feel about my errand yesterday, though it does seem it isn't my own, but rather Master's, as doing his bidding is only my duty. Still it *was* my half-day and I'd a perfect right to refuse, though such a course never come to me for a moment until after the whole thing was concluded. I dressed and went down to the kitchen, hoping to be at my work before Cook come in, but of course she was there and would ask at once how my day had gone and if I'd found the cloth for my cloak, so I had to sit over my tea and lie about going to this store or that, but nothing would do. Lying does not come easy to me, nor do I do it well. I thought Cook looked at me close, and felt myself blushing with confusion. Then Mr. Poole come in and said Master had been in his laboratory the entire night and had just come in and wanted his breakfast and fire and then to be left alone, as he intended to sleep until noon, he was that done in. Cook turned to her pans and I put on my bonnet and apron, feeling grateful to have the opportunity to deliver my message so early in the day. Mr. Bradshaw came in and he and Mr. Poole sat down at the table to wait on their own breakfast. "I'll do the fire now," I said and went off feeling disapproval in the air, though this was likely my own imagining as there was nothing uncommon in my actions.

I went up the stairs and knocked at Master's door.

He called out to me, I went in and found him, as I expected, lying on his bed in his dressing gown. "I've come to do your fire," I said, and he only responded, "Yes, good," so I went straight to work, hardly having looked at him. My heart was pounding, as if I had something to fear, and I went over and over sentences that would be the answers to his questions, how I had fared on his errand, what Mrs. Farraday had said, sentences that would tell him how distrustful and sad I felt so that he would explain to me the meaning of it all and set my mind at rest.

When I stood up and turned to him I saw he was lying back on his pillows with his eyes closed, looking for all the world like a corpse, pale and drawn about the temples. My heart sank, for I knew I couldn't speak and I stood near the foot of the bed gazing at him stupidly.

His eyelids flickered, he saw that I was there, but he seemed too weak to take me in, so he closed them again, turning his head a little away from me. I thought I should have to go away and speak to him at some later time, but just as I was making up my mind to go out he spoke, still without looking at me. "Were you able to deliver my letter for me, Mary?" he said.

"I did, sir," I said.

"And the answer?"

My poor head seemed about to burst. I knew I could not say any of the sentences I had thought out so careful. I couldn't even bring myself to say the name of Mrs. Farraday, much less tell my feelings of shock and concern for Master, that she should speak of him so disrespectful and talk to me, too, as she had, so rude, seeing as I was connected to him and to his house. I heard myself say only, "The answer is yes, sir, though she says you must wait two weeks."

Master sighed. "Good," he said. "That will be quite convenient." Nor did he turn toward me or even open his eyes, seeming to be nearly asleep, and so I went out.

I went down the stairs feeling as weary as if I had worked all day, instead of as I should after my half-day, refreshed and ready to shine up a palace if the chance arose. In the kitchen Cook was just putting out some eggs and rashers. I took my plate with a heavy heart and sat down next to Mr. Bradshaw, who was in a jovial mood, teasing me about my young man in the park, with whom I must be spending my half-day pretty "vigorous," as he put it, for I seemed worn out in his view.

I only looked up from my food to say, with my whole heart behind it, "Mr. Bradshaw, I do wish that was the truth," and we all had a dry laugh at my expense.

*T*wo weeks has passed since last I writ, and I thought this morning that today is the day Master's business with Mrs. Farraday must begin. I have spent many hours trying to coach myself on what that business might be, and I think I must have a good imagination when I consider just how many stories I've come up with, some to Master's credit and some that shock me for having appeared in my own head. Indeed I am in a bad way and weary from it all. Master is occupied much of the time, in his laboratory or visiting or having his friends in, and seems to think on those occasions when I am in the room with him that everything is as it has always been. I try to believe this myself and do my work with a good will, but I don't believe it no matter how much I might try.

It does seem to me that what Master has done is take rooms in that house, or perhaps the whole house, and that he has done this for someone else, someone Mrs. Farraday (if that is her name, for I doubt everything in my worst moments) knows and does not like.

The only thing I do that lifts my spirits is work in the garden with Cook. We have managed several times to get in an hour in the early morning, or late in the day as the days is so long now, and many of our plants has their heads above the soil. Now an hour of work can make a noticeable order. The weather has been grey, unseasonable cold and wet, the coldest summer in many years, but our herbs and flowers seem to thrive upon it. We have parsley of two kinds—one curly, which Cook says she will use for garnish, and one with a flat leaf for cooking—rosemary, thyme, mint—a most hardy plant this is, as goes underground to jump up again in a space not its own, which Cook says is the nuisance of it and if we went away the whole garden would be only mint in no time—sage, garlic, and marigolds to prevent bugs, one border of pansies, not bloomed yet, and another of poppies, which are just coming up and so delicate I fear they won't prosper, and two edges, one of lavender and one of foxglove. Cook has a little place in the centre for a boxwood, which she is looking out for, she says, as a present for me because it will bring a good marriage.

Nothing is big enough to pick yet but we can see how it will look. There's a deal of feeding and pinching and always weeding to be done, which Cook directs me in.

Sometimes, if I'm not too busy, I go out after dinner just to look at it, and to smell the pleasant scent of the herbs which the damp air seems to blend into something that is all one, though I feel I can separate out each herb if I try. Yesterday as I was doing this, feeling it really is a blessing at such times to have a nose, though at others one may wish to close up a nose as we do our eyes when we don't want to see, I heard Master passing along the closed passage that leads to the side street. I knew it must be Master as the passage has only one other door, which opens into the old theatre, yet the step did not sound like his but rather too heavy and uneven, dragging a little. Still, it must have been him, only my ears misled me or the hard flags of the passage mun distort the sound. He went along from the theatre, opened the door to the street, then went out.

Why did this surprise me so, and why did I have a feeling of such gloom at the thought that Master comes and goes in his own house without our always knowing? Certain it would be unnecessary steps and trouble to cross the yard and walk through the house to the front door when this door is so much the more convenient.

But, I thought, how much of the time that we think Master is in his laboratory, not to be disturbed, is he perhaps not there at all?

I stood still, listening, but there were no sounds, then a fine rain began to fall and the sound of it seemed to fill up my head so that I couldn't move. I hoped Master had remembered to take his umbrella—a foolish thought, but it seemed important and I went over it a few times as if thinking on it could put the umbrella in his hands. And I was getting wet myself but didn't care. I looked down at my hands, which no matter how I scrub them are always lined with blacking and lately, because of the odd weather, have been full of twinges and pains that feel like hearts throbbing. I remembered what seemed like so long ago, when Master took my hands in his own and looked at them in the lamplight, of how shy and embarrassed I felt, but yet, I cannot deny it, pleased as well to be noticed by him, to feel I was of interest to him. As I was having these sad thoughts Mr. Poole put his head out the kitchen door and called to me. "Mary," he said. "Have you no more sense than to stand there dreaming in the rain?" I went in, thinking how I must seem to Mr. Poole, who knows nothing of me, and less of Master than he could ever suspect, I've no doubt.

his morning I was polishing the tables in the drawing room, in fact on my knees on the floor to do the legs which stand on great carved animal feet I like to think is lion's feet, when Master come in suddenly and seeming in a hurry, threw himself down on the settee so that his long legs stretched out before him on the carpet, and heaved a great sigh as if he was at the end of a struggle. Then he saw me, or rather saw the back of me and said, "Mary, good. You are the person who should hear of this."

So I had to back out from under the table and turn myself around to him on my knees. Then I thought it wouldn't do to stand, as he was nearly lying down, so I sat back on my heels and said, "Yes, sir."

"It's inconceivable to me," he went on. "They want to close my school."

"I'm sorry to hear that, sir," I said.

"The commissioners are of the opinion that educating the poor is a dangerous pastime."

"I can't see how that could be," I said.

"It seems two of our scholars haven't done very well, though we can't say they didn't profit, for they got themselves up to be assistants at the school and then disappeared with all the funds they could lay their hands upon." Here Master laughed abruptly, rolling his eyes upward as if he'd never heard of anything so ridiculous.

"That's a pity, sir," I said, "if it makes your friends feel their good effort has come to a bad end."

"They say we've only taught pickpockets to be embezzlers."

"Surely sir," I said, "they must expect something like that now and then."

"Exactly what I told them. Naturally we must lose a few along the way, but why does that lead to the conclusion that we should give up the whole enterprise? And I brought you up, Mary, as an example of one who has come through our school with her moral capabilities intact. I told them my housemaid can read and write as well as any of you, and I've no doubt is a far better critic of reason and morality than any of you seem to be."

This made me blush and I could only stammer, "You flatter me, sir."

"No, Mary, I don't, and you'd agree with me if you had five minutes of conversation with these fools. Littleton, whose name is surely a description of the size and density of his brain, said he for one wouldn't care to have a housemaid with any moral sense at all—and the whole group of asses brayed out loud over that for a full minute."

"I'm sorry to hear that, sir," I said.

"I'm not so naïve as to think we can solve the world's problems by having a school, but surely we've an obligation to relieve suffering when we can. And ignorance *is* suffering, though the poor brutes who are driven to our doors may not know it. Any school, simply by existing, must be a force for good."

I smiled, both at the excitement in Master's speech

and the strange idea he'd brought to my mind. "What makes you smile, Mary?" he said at once. "Am I wrong? Speak frankly."

"I was thinking that there can never be such a thing as a force for good, sir," I said. "And there's the pity of it."

Master opened his eyes wide and protested, "But, Mary, I try to be just such a force."

"Well that's it, sir, isn't it," I said. "That good is what always needs trying, as it is work for us and don't seem to come natural, whereas havoc comes of its own accord. And also it does seem to me that the two words won't go together, as force can never do aught but evil."

Master paused, mulling over my words. "Surely this is a grim view, Mary. If this is true then we must despair of our efforts—indeed, there is no point in any effort."

"Oh, I suppose, sir," I said, "it does little harm to try. Your wicked boys is really no wickeder for learning to rob a school instead of a pocket."

Master smiled. "And it seems to me also, Mary, that there are many who have no difficulty in being good. Yourself, for example."

"Being and doing is different, sir," I said. "I have no will to cause pain and suffering, as some do, if that's what you mean. But as for *doing* good, I confess I don't think of it. I only think of doing what I mun to stay as I am."

"Which *is* good," Master said, as if to pay me a compliment.

But my answer sprang to my lips, and I knew Master mun understand it as no one else might.

"No, sir," I said. "Which is safe."

Master leaned forward, propping his chin on one hand and gave me a long look, full of sympathy, so that there was no need to speak. We heard, though only because we had fallen silent, Mr. Poole's step in the hall, for he walks like a ghost and often as not appears in a doorway as if he just sprang up from the floorboards. Master and I exchanged a look of warning, for if Mr. Poole saw me on my knees talking to Master, he would not approve and Master knows this as well as I. I went back to my lion's feet and Master fell back on the settee. In the next moment Mr. Poole looked in, seeming surprised to see Master, and said, "Ah, sir, I did not know you had come in."

*I*t is very late. I'm weary but won't sleep I know until I puzzle out my poor feelings, which has been in an uproar all day so that there is a chorus of voices in my head, each one demanding to be heard against the others. When Master is gay and kind to me, as he was today, asking my opinion and listening to me as no one has ever listened to me, then all the sadness I feel lifts as suddenly as a bird, leaves me entirely, and I know such a soaring of spirits as I think mun come to few in this life. Though I tell myself this is only a gentleman having idle conversation with his housemaid for want of a better pastime, I don't believe it, have no will to believe it, but respond, no, he wants *my* company and not another's. When he talks to me of doing good, of how his efforts is blocked by those who only think of money or prestige, then my worry about his sending me out on an errand to Soho, my distrust of the woman he has chosen to help him, seems the worst sort of suspicious mind, to imagine that Master means anything but good or that he owes me some explanation of his intentions. I feel ashamed of myself and resolve to accept my place as *Master* makes it out for me, and not as I might want it to be. When he tells me he trusts me and shows me he trusts me more than anyone else in this house, my heart leaps and I think, I am of use to him and mun keep that trust, that my obligation is clear, yet there is another voice that will put in, he means nothing by it, he is gay and it pleases him to say such things to one who cannot but obey him. This, I've no doubt, is Mr. Poole's view of the matter and though he says nothing to me, his coolness is such as mun be felt by everyone in the house, except, of course, for Master, who cares nothing about it. When I went down to the kitchen after speaking with Master this morning, Mr. Poole was sitting at the table with Mr. Bradshaw, who did not fail to notice the cold look he gave me as I come in or the tone of his words to me, which was to suggest that I find a way to do the drawing room in the afternoon, when it is less likely to be in use.

There. I hear Master coming in from his laboratory, climbing through the dark, still house and thinking we are all of us asleep in our beds while he is left alone, awake. Can he feel that I am here, listening to him, sleepless on his account? Will he think of me as he goes into his room, lights the lamp I trimmed for him, sits on the bed I made for him, drinks the water I brought up for him, or perhaps lights the fire I laid for him and stands gazing at the burning coals until sleep finally finds us both?

After we finished our tea today, Mr. Poole had a bell to the drawing room, but come back at once to say that Master had asked we all gather in Mr. Poole's parlour, as he wished to speak to us as a group. Of course we was all taken by surprise, Cook saying it mun be something serious and perhaps Master had suffered a reverse in fortunes and couldn't keep so grand a house, which had happened to her in her last position, but Mr. Poole told her to hold her tongue as no such thing was likely, only Master mun want some small change in the running of things, or perhaps he was going abroad.

So we put up the tea things quickly, Mr. Poole opened his parlour door and we all filed in—Cook, Mr. Bradshaw, Annie, myself, Mr. Poole, and the knife boy, Peter, who was very nervous as this is his first position and he is scarce more than a child and shan't find another with ease. We stood about, not wanting to take seats nor feeling we should be together in a group nor queued up, so we milled about the table, giving each other worried looks and Cook said she did not like it at all.

At length we heard Master's step on the staircase and he appeared at the door, seeming as he did yesterday, pressed but in good spirits, and he looked from one to another of us and said, "Good, here you all are."

Mr. Poole, who was propped against a china cabinet said in his stiffest manner, "We are all eager to hear what you have to tell us, sir."

Master looked at Cook, who had really gone white and was clutching at the back of a chair, and he said, "Good heavens, I'd say eager was the wrong word, Poole. Poor Mrs. Kent looks as though she may fall down." Then he laughed and went to Cook, pulling out a chair for her, which she fell into obediently. "Please sit down, all of you," Master said. "And be assured I haven't called you together to deal some crushing blow. My news is rather indifferent and should cause no change, no change at all, dear Mrs. Kent, in the duties you all discharge so faithfully."

We took seats around the table, except for Mr.

Poole who took the chair before his desk and turned it so that he faced Master but none of us could see him.

"As you all know," Master said—"as you, Mary, have often told me" (here I was glad I could not see Mr. Poole's expression, though I was sure I felt his eyes burning into the back of my head)—"my work in the laboratory consumes so much of my time and energy that I scarcely have enough of either to carry it out. Indeed I cannot carry it out as efficiently as I would like, so after much thinking and searching about, I have decided to take an assistant." Here Master paused, as if we might have some comment, which we had not. I was thinking it very odd that Master should do such a thing. It irritated me to hear it, though I couldn't say why, even to myself.

"I inform you all of this decision," Master went on, "because it is important to me, and to my work, that this young man, Mr. Edward Hyde, have complete liberty in my house as well as in my laboratory, and that you all treat him with the respect and diligence in service that you show me."

As we all sat in dumb silence, Mr. Poole put in, "You may rely on it, sir."

"Good, then. I'll say no more about it. Honestly I think he will have little to do in the house, and will for the most part confine his work to the laboratory, but I want to be sure he can come and go freely without occasioning any disturbance in your minds—and, of course, should he require your assistance I want you all to have the assurance that he has, by my wish, the same authority I have."

I found myself looking at Cook, who seemed to lose interest in Master's remarks once she knew they did not mean anything must change in her own domain, so that while she kept her eyes raised attentively to Master, her hands was busy smoothing out her apron across her lap, running one finger along the hem, I thought, looking for a loose thread. I wanted to look at Mr. Poole, who was, I had no doubt, not pleased with the notion of a young man who might order him about or in some way disturb the routine of our house, but I couldn't turn around to do so. It made me smile to think of it, and of how he must be making a nice bland face for Master's benefit while underneath his thoughts was all havoc, and I looked up at Master to see he had stopped speaking and was looking right at me, smiling at me with an expression of amusement—almost, I thought, of affection, that I blushed to be receiving it in front of my fellows.

"Good, then," Master said without taking his eyes off me. "I will rely on you all, as I always do." Then he went out and we heard him going up the stairs with a quick step. We all sat for a moment without speaking until Cook said, "Well, I don't suppose he'll be wanting his meals here," and Mr. Poole replied quickly, "No, I shouldn't think so." We got up, pushing in our chairs, and went back to our duties, each, I have no doubt, trying to imagine the face and manner of this new, this young master, Mr. Edward Hyde.

*A*t dinner Mr. Bradshaw and Mr. Poole talked over Master's announcement while the rest of us listened like dumb animals. Mr. Bradshaw, who has been here five years, wondered if Master ever needed such help before and Mr. Poole, who never tires of reminding us he has been here twenty, pointed out that no such person had been required for twenty years. Mr. Poole had plenty of ideas about why such a plan would appeal to Master now. First, his humanitarian work, of which he and Mr. Poole are justly proud, takes up more of his time than previously, so that he has less time for his researches and mun work into the night, as we see, endangering his health. Second, Master is getting to be elderly and it might reasonably occur to him that if his work is to proceed, there mun be some person who can understand it and carry it on in his absence. Third, and this one surprised me, Master is a bachelor and a wealthy one, without an heir. He has perhaps found some young gentleman who can serve as both an assistant and the eventual recipient of *all* Master's concerns, and Master wants to have him about as much as possible, to be sure he has made the right choice.

Mr. Bradshaw agreed with all this and wondered if the assistant was actually in Master's employ, as we were, or would he be more of a reliable friend to our Master, to be treated, for example, as his solicitor, Mr. Utterson.

Mr. Poole said this was a delicate question and the

answer mun in some part depend upon the young man's situation. He did feel that this assistant, whether he be paid or no, was clearly in Master's mind by no means a servant, as he was to have perfect liberty in the house. Mr. Bradshaw, who will tease, said that it seemed to him Mr. Poole had perfect liberty in the house, so how could this young man have more.

Mr. Poole puffed up and bristled. He can never tell when Mr. Bradshaw is joking or no, though the rest of us can, and said that he understood Master's wish to be that we should all be prepared to take orders from this Mr. Hyde and that he was himself fully ready to do so.

Then they fell silent and Cook said again she did not like it, but supposed she mun make the best of it. That was the end of our discussion.

After dinner Mr. Poole went into his parlour and closed the door. Mr. Bradshaw went off to his room while Cook and I sat at the table drinking our beer and poor Annie did the rough business of scouring her pots. Suddenly the door opened and Mr. Poole looked in on us, scowling mightily, and said, "Mary, I'd like a word with you before you go up," so I bolted my glass and went in at once, he following me, closing the door on Cook and Annie, who must have wondered what terrible thing I had done, though I thought I knew it and I was right. Mr. Poole took his seat at his desk and I stood before him, my hands folded under my apron, for all the world like a child caught out and feeling it too.

"I feel I must tell you, Mary, that your behaviour in

this house is perplexing, even distressing to me, and a remark Dr. Jekyll made in his talk to us today has made me think it must fall to me to direct you in your duties, as he, evidently out of kindness, has not done so."

"Yes, sir," I said.

"Do you have an idea what I'm speaking of?" he asked, trying to get me to accuse myself of something, I've no doubt, which made me so weary I decided to have done with it as soon as possible.

"I believe I do," I said. This surprised him a little, I saw, which pleased me.

"And what is your idea?"

"That Master said I told him he taxed his health with working so much at his researches, and that it was not my place to have spoken to him on such a subject."

"Well, that is it, of course, Mary. And how do you feel about having done so?"

"That I was too forward, sir, and won't ever be so again."

Then he was silent, and looked me up and down impatient. I could feel how much he does not like me, but I kept my eyes down, for I knew if I looked at him my feelings would be in my face and then he would find some way to get rid of me altogether.

"We are all of us concerned for Dr. Jekyll's health, Mary," he said. "None more so than another. We can show our concern by making his house run smoothly and not increasing his burden with calling attention to our opinions."

I could think of no answer to this as it did not

contain a question but was rather his way of driving home a point, so I stood looking at the carpet.

At last he said, "That's all I have to say for the present, Mary. You may go."

"Yes, sir," I said. "Thank you, sir," and I went out, straight past Cook and Annie and up to my room, as if I had been punished, feeling at each step a great weight of despair settling over me, for if Mr. Poole decides he is my enemy, he will see to it that Master cannot be my friend.

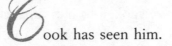ook has seen him.

She went out to the market early this morning and as she came round the corner she saw him hurrying along the street. The sun was hardly up, the lamps was still lit and the fog so thick, as it has been these three days, that she said he seemed to come out of the black as if he was made of it. At first she paid him no heed, as she does not look at every stranger on the street, but then she saw he was holding a key and his eye was bent on the passage door to Master's laboratory, so she stopped to have a good look at him.

She told us this at breakfast, when Mr. Poole was out at the chemist's, for he would not like us gossiping about Master's assistant, though I'm sure he's as curious as we. "What sort of gentleman is he?" Mr. Bradshaw asked.

"Why, it's hard to say," Cook replied. "I saw him so sudden and then he was in at the door and never did see me. But he's a very small gentleman, hardly taller than you, Mary; in fact he may not be as tall" (which I thought must mean he is small indeed as I am not tall by anyone's measuring and rarely see a man smaller than myself). "But he's not slight, nor heavy."

"Well," said Mr. Bradshaw. "Now, that's a clear picture, Mrs. Kent. He is small but not small."

"I believe he is stooped a little," said Cook. "Or perhaps his legs is too short for the rest of him."

"Well," Mr. Bradshaw said. "Is he a dwarf?"

"No," said Cook. "Not a dwarf, but something odd about him."

"Did you see his face?" Annie put in, to my surprise, for Annie rarely has the energy to wonder about anything.

"Only in shadow," Cook said. "I could make out that he is dark and his hair is long, curly, coarse stuff, more of it than most gentlemen would care for. He is clean-shaven and he was well dressed, though he looked the worse for wear to me and I had the feeling he had not changed but was coming in straight from a night out."

"That won't set well with his new employer," Mr. Bradshaw said. "Perhaps he won't last long."

Then we was silent, for we heard Mr. Poole coming in at the door, but I thought we was all of the same feeling and Mr. Bradshaw had said what we wished was true. Master's assistant has not been in the house at all and already we was bothered with him. I put my plate away and went out to fill my buckets, as I wanted to get the front steps done, but when I got there it hardly seemed worth the effort as the fog was so thick I could scarcely see across the yard, so it seemed unlikely anyone would *see* our steps, yet such work must be done regular. When my buckets was filled I set to tying up my skirts, for I don't care to drag them about in the water, though I've seen others as don't seem to mind and would rather be soaked to the knees than have their ankles exposed, which seems like false modesty to me, and as I did this I heard the theatre door open and someone step out into the yard. It struck me at once that now I was to see Mr. Edward Hyde, though I could make out nothing yet for the fog, and I felt it awkward to meet him thus—even, I think, I was annoyed. Then I heard a few steps going toward the house and I thought, no, that is Master's step. A moment later my question was answered for I heard a clatter, then Master's voice said, "Damn!" quite sudden and distressed. Without thinking I ran towards the sound to find Master on his hands and knees, having tripped over a raised bit of flag and gone down completely.

"Lord, sir," I said. "Have you hurt yourself?"

Master rolled over sideways, then sat up, his legs stretched out before him. "I think I have, Mary," he said. "I heard my ankle snap as I fell."

"Don't move, sir," I said. "Shall I go for Mr. Poole?"

"No," Master said. "Let me just sit a moment and see what I've done. I think it may be only a sprain."

"Shall I take off your shoe?"

Master laughed. "If you can find it in this soup, Mary, yes I suppose we should have a look at it. It's my right foot."

I knelt down at Master's feet and began unlacing his boot, pulling the leather apart carefully and grasping it by the heel to pull it off as easy as I could, but still it made Master moan, "Oh."

"Should I go for a doctor?" I said. "Perhaps it is broken, sir."

"I believe we have a doctor in the house," Master said, which made me laugh.

"I'm sorry, sir," I said. "I wasn't thinking."

"Just hold it by the heel," Master said. "And move the foot in a circle very gently, Mary, then I can tell what I've done."

I did as he bid me, feeling nervous as it seemed I mun be hurting him, but he was silent, then said, "That's enough. It's not so bad, I think, but I won't be able to walk on it." I was kneeling on the flags and I let Master's foot rest in my lap, wondering what we should do to get him into the house; though I felt I was strong enough to support him if he was willing to lean upon me, still it seemed it was for Master to decide. We was both of us looking at his poor foot, which I was thinking really is so long and slender, I could feel the bones through the stocking and it seemed to me they was too fine to carry a man of Master's height. Then I looked up to see Master was looking at me and I felt shy because I did not have on my bonnet or apron and my hair had come loose, so I smoothed it back with my hands and said, "I was just getting my buckets for the front steps."

Master's face was pale and he bit his lip as I spoke, so I thought he must be in pain and should be in his bed. The fog was around us so thick that we could not see the house or the theatre door and seemed to be in a world of cloud, as if we'd fallen into the sky. "How strange I feel," Master said. "I think I must lie down," and with that he lay back on the damp flags and closed his eyes, but continued to speak to me. "Just for a moment, Mary," he said. "Then with your help I'll go into the house. I did not sleep last night and this fall has taken whatever there was left of me."

This made me feel helpless and I thought, if Master cannot even sit up I shall never get him in, he is too big for me. Then I thought his assistant mun still be in the laboratory, as Cook had seen him go in, and surely Master would want him to know of his condition. I said, "Sir, you are in a bad way. Shall I go for your assistant?"

Master's eyes flew open. He rose up on his elbows and gave me a wondering look. "My assistant?" he said. "No, he isn't here."

"Oh," was all I said, not wanting Master to know

how we all sat about talking the moment one of us had a look at the man.

"Mary," Master said. "I must get to my room. If you will stand here and allow me to lean upon you, I think it can be accomplished."

So I jumped up and Master got himself up on one foot. Then he put one arm across my shoulder and I, feeling awkward at first, put my hand across his back. In this way we got into the hall door, then he used the rail to get upstairs while I hovered along beside him. At the top he leaned upon me again and we got down the hall to his room. He collapsed in his armchair near the fire, looking so white and shaken I feared he would faint, but he only put his head back on the cushion with a sigh and said, "I can manage from here, Mary. But I must ask you to go and fetch my boot."

"Yes, sir," I said. "I'll bring it here." I went out and down the stairs in a hurry, though there was not much need for it as neither Master nor the boot was likely to go anywhere. I stepped out into the yard, thinking of what was done for such an injury—was it best to soak it in hot water or perhaps wrap it up in bandages to keep it from moving?—which was useless for me to think on as I know nothing about such matters and Master surely does, so I walked out into the yard and discovered the fog was still so thick I could not see Master's boot. It seemed my head was up in the fog but when I looked down I could see my own feet plain enough, so I thought I must kneel down and look under the fog. This I did, looking towards the theatre where I thought it must be, but I didn't find it. So I turned towards the house and there it was, but I felt a strange thud in my chest for it was on the other side of the garden.

I felt sure I had not crossed the garden to get to Master, though I could have, by running between the edge and the house; still, it just did not seem to me to be right and I felt sure that Master had fallen on the near side from where I was kneeling. But I told myself I mun be mistaken. No one would move the boot even if someone had come into the yard, for what would be the purpose of it, so I went quickly and picked it up, chiding myself as such things happen often in a fog as thick as this one was, and one cannot even be sure of *hearing* correctly, so that a voice may seem far away when it is really near. Then, as if to prove this, I heard a voice call my name, "Mary," as if it was next to my ear. It startled me so, I stood clutching Master's boot to my chest and I felt my skin go so cold that drops of moisture formed on my forehead. What direction am I facing, I asked myself, the house or Master's laboratory? And I did not know whether to run or stand still, but turned around slowly on the flags until it came again, "Mary," sharp, but this time I recognized it. I said, "Mr. Bradshaw, I am here."

"Come in, then," he said, more friendly, as it is not his way to be cool to his fellows, and I followed his voice in through the fog. "The master has hurt himself," he said, "and Mr. Poole is looking everywhere for you."

*N*othing is as it should be. Master would not stay in his bed one day but he was up and hobbling about with a walking stick, saying he could neglect his work no longer, so after lunch yesterday he struck out across the yard to his laboratory and did not come back. Though he'd got no orders, Mr. Poole had Cook make up a dinner tray and brought it out. Then he came back looking perplexed, saying Master must have fallen asleep in his cabinet, as he didn't answer, so he'd left the tray at the door. We had our own dinner and tidied up. I did a bit of sewing downstairs while Cook went over her shopping lists and Mr. Poole closed himself up in his parlour, the three of us too anxious to go to bed, though it is not that uncommon for Master to go off, still there was something not right about it. We sat up until nearly eleven waiting to hear Master come in, but he did not. Just before I went up, I made an excuse that I'd forgotten to bring in my brushes (which was true enough, I had forgot) so I went out into the yard. We have finally a little summer with us and it was warm, very damp, the air pressing all round, full of scents from the garden, so it was pleasant to stand still and look about, letting my eyes grow used to the dark. I looked up at the blank wall of Master's laboratory. The big door made a patch of black against the grey stone, and it seemed if I looked at it hard enough I could make it open and Master come out, for I was filled with some fear for him and the wall was to me like a blank, eyeless face, full of secrets. Of course he did not come, so at last I went in and put up my brushes. Cook looked up at me as if she thought I might have seen something, but I only said good night to her and climbed the long steps feeling I should never have the strength to get to the top. I fell asleep straight away and did not wake up until nearly morning. There was just that dull glow to the air before light comes and, as the window was open, the rustling of the birds even came to me, otherwise the world was very still. Yet I felt something had waked me and in the next moment I knew what it was. Someone was walking quickly across the yard, in at the kitchen door without a pause and then up the back stairs. It is Master, I thought, but I knew at once it was not, for Master's injury would not let him move so quick. Then I knew this was the same step I had heard before, in the passage, light but dragging somehow. I sat up in the bed. Annie lay beside me, her back to me, but I knew there was not much chance of her being awake. I sat straining my ears to hear and one of the things that seemed very loud was my own heart. The footsteps went up to the first floor, but then not, as I expected, on up to Master's room, but rather very directly, knowing his way it seemed to me, without a pause to Master's drawing room.

This cannot be right, I thought. I must go down and see what this is about. I put my legs over the side of the bed and stood up, feeling shaky, but I scolded myself, saying, what have you to fear, you must only go down and knock on Mr. Bradshaw's door. Then I came so much to myself that I thought, you cannot call Mr. Bradshaw out in your night shift, so I took my old cloak from the peg and wrapped myself in it. In this time I heard the intruder open a drawer, then fall silent.

This is such boldness as will be met, I thought, and quick as I could I opened the door, made my way down to the landing, quiet and fast as possible, then stopped. Now the footsteps had begun again. He was leaving the drawing room, running to the stairs, and in a moment would be gone. If I hurried down the next flight I might run into him.

I cast a hopeless look at the door to Master's bedroom. Was he there? Had he come in without my hearing? Now my heart was thudding, for the footsteps was just below me. He was on the landing beneath mine and if I took one step forward he would look up to see me standing above him. Indeed he was not moving but seemed to have paused on the landing, waiting for me to make myself known. I felt he *would* be known, that he willed me to take that one step, yet I could not take it. Rather I stepped back, leaning against the wall to hold myself up, feeling my mouth go dry and my knees give way, so that my only thought was, don't fall. In that moment he hurried down the stairs while I sank down onto the carpet, my face in my hands. I heard the kitchen door open, then close. Wave after wave of fear flowed over me and it was strange, for I knew he was gone and I had nothing more to fear. But I was crouched on the floor, quivering, trying to make myself small and cursing the tears in my eyes. He always hated me to cry, it enraged him more than anything I could do and I always paid for it if he saw me. I had the thought that came to me so often as a child, when I heard him coming for me, when he was in the room, but I hadn't the courage to look up and see where, because if I kept myself small I hoped he would not notice me. So I thought, oh please, oh please, don't let him see me, don't let him think of me.

Who was it I pleaded with?

After a time I came to myself, dried my eyes and remembered where I was. The window over the landing is of stained glass and the dim morning light cast spots of red, like pools of blood, on the carpet, on my hands. I did not get up at once but sat giving myself some counsel. First I told myself this intruder must surely be Master's assistant, as he came in with no difficulty, so he must have a key, and though it was an odd hour to be in our house, doubtless he was on some mission for Master. I got up, straightened my cloak over my shoulders and went downstairs quietly, for in another hour the house would be awake and many as sleep light in that last hour—I know I do. I went to the drawing room, which was dark as the curtains was still drawn, and I stood in the doorway looking to see if anything was amiss. Master's desk under the window was open and the drawer pulled out. For some reason this gave me a shudder. I went to look at it and found Master's big book of cheques lying open, the pen next it—not in the holder, as Master always leaves it, but laid aside and dripping ink onto the blotter. Without thinking I righted the pen, closed the book and slipped it into the drawer. Then I thought perhaps I should not have touched it.

But most of all I thought why is Mr. Edward Hyde, for surely it was he, writing cheques in Master's own cheque-book at such an hour and in such a hurry?

I closed the desk and turned my back on it, feeling so uneasy it was as if I turned my back on a bad dog who might suddenly knock me sprawling, so I fairly crept out of the drawing room and up the stairs. On the landing I stopped and looked again at the door to Master's bedroom.

Was he asleep behind it?

I knew he was not, though how I knew I cannot say. Nor why I felt then such anger and such boldness to do the strange thing I did. I went to the door and rapped softly upon it, having no idea what I would say if Master called out for me to enter, for I knew he would not. Then I opened the door, slowly at first, until I could see the big bed, empty and neatly made up, as I had done it that morning. In a moment I entered the room and closed the door behind me. I know every inch of Master's room, for I have cleaned it often enough, yet it seemed to me I was in a strange place full of secrets. Perhaps it was the light, which was very dim, though I could see my way about easily enough. The windows was open and the lace curtain puffed in a little from the breeze, which was warm, very damp. Soon it would be raining, I could smell that in the air.

How odd I felt! How odd I was! I went to Master's shaving mirror and looked at my face in the glass. My hair was down and wild around my face, which looked very pale and vexed to me, and my eyes seemed bright, no doubt from being washed by tears. I saw there was two lines in my forehead and I rubbed at them. I dropped my cloak on the carpet to look at my neck and shoulders—also, it seemed to me, too pale even against the white of my night shift. But my shoulders and arms are strong, from the heavy work I do, especially getting the coal up, and it gave me a little pleasure to see that though I am small, I do look strong and healthy. I would have looked in the cheval glass but it is gone to Master's cabinet where even now, I thought, perhaps Master is looking up from his work to see himself, or Mr. Edward Hyde who has come running in with a cheque. That fancy vexed me so that I turned away from the glass and stood looking at Master's bed. It is a fine piece—heavy, dark, carved with strange fruits and flowers across the headboard, which is high, and the footboard, also higher than most, I think, with feet that look like a bird's claw holding onto a ball of gleaming wood. Whenever I am polishing it, or making it up, or turning the mattress, I cannot but admire it. I felt so bold then that I went over to it and smoothed the coverlet, then rested my cheek against it. All my fear was vanished, and even it seemed most of my sense, for at the thought that Mr. Poole might come in and see me in my shift, swooning over Master's bed, I had to hold down a laugh.

Then I stood up still, thinking I might be heard, that even my bare feet on the carpet must give me away if I so much as made a move for the door. I leaned against the bed, looking at the room around me, Master's shaving basin, the fireplace—cold now, for it had not been lit since the day before—the wine-coloured chair he sometimes draws up before it, the pictures on the walls, all drawings and paintings of scenes, all in heavy, dark frames, the heavy, winy curtains with the lace beneath rustling in the breeze. Then a sadness come over me and I felt I was sinking very low, from my fear on the stairs and the memories stirred up of being hunted and noplace to hide. I thought, I cannot live if I am not to feel safe in *this* house, with *this* master, who has cared for me and talked to me, who values me as no one ever has. If I must cringe and weep in *this* house, then what will become of me?

I put on my cloak, which I wrapped around me tight, for I felt cold of a sudden and weak, and went out as quiet as I could, down the hall and up to my room. Annie was asleep and in a moment I slipped in beside her, where I lay still but not sleeping, until a long hour had passed and it was time to get up and go about my work.

We all of us spent the morning in a bad temper, airing rooms, polishing silver, brushing clothes, cleaning pots, keeping a house for a master who is not there. Mr. Poole went out and came back with Master's dinner tray which had not been touched. It is warm and the fires in the hall and drawing room has been down these two days, so I made up my mind to take advantage of it. After lunch I dressed in my oldest apron, took up my brushes and polish, and set to cleaning and blacking the grates, getting out all the ashes in scuttles, a job which makes me as black as a sweep. I was halfway up the chimney in the hall when Mr. Bradshaw scared me out of my wits by touching me on the back, but when I saw his face I could not be annoyed, for he looked as if he was the one who had had a shock.

"Mary," he said. "You'd best give that up and come into the kitchen at once. Master has come in a bad way."

So I straightened myself as best I could, though there was nothing to be done about the black but try to keep it off the carpet as I went along, and followed Mr. Bradshaw to the kitchen.

Master sat sprawled at the table, looking more dead than alive. When I come into the room he looked up at me as if he did not know me. In fact, he seemed hardly to know he was in his own house. Mr. Poole stood over him like a mother hen, and Cook was on his other side, but they seemed not to know what to do. Cook said to me, "I don't know how he got across the yard. He can scarce walk." His stick lay on the floor where, I thought, he must have dropped it, seeing that the table might hold him up. His clothes was awry, the collar undone, nor did he have on his coat, and I saw the cuff on his shirt was only half fastened, as if he'd put it on in a hurry. He put his head down in his arms and groaned. Mr. Poole seemed to recollect himself at that and began giving orders all round, to Cook to get some water boiling, to me to prepare Master's bed, and to Mr. Bradshaw to help support Master up the stairs.

I took off my apron, brushed myself as best I could and cleaned my hands quickly in a bucket. Master lifted his head to say, "My boot. Please take it off," and Cook said, "His poor ankle. He has done it in now."

Mr. Poole told Cook to hold her tongue and then got on his knees to take off Master's boots. I watched long enough to see that Master's ankle was twice the size it should be and so tender that Mr. Poole said he must cut the sock off with a scissors. So I went ahead up the stairs to prepare the room.

The room was warm and damp to my way of thinking, but I knew Master would find it chilly so I closed the window at once. Then I turned back the bed and laid out Master's dressing gown, filled the basin with water and opened the door to his dressing room. I could hear them on the stairs, helping him along. In a moment they were at the door, Master between Mr. Bradshaw and Mr. Poole, hopping on one foot with his head dropped forward as if he could not hold it up. They set him down on his chair so clumsily I thought he would fall right out of it, but the jolt seemed to wake him up and he looked about, seeming very weary but relieved. Mr. Bradshaw went off and Mr. Poole took the scissors from the dresser and fell to cutting off Master's sock.

"I'd like a fire, Mary," Master said, though he did not look at me but at his ankle, which was now exposed and was indeed such a sorry sight, swollen and bruised many colours so that we all of us could do nothing but stare at it and I said, "Lord, sir, sure it is broken now."

But Master said, "No, only I should not have been on it so soon." Mr. Poole took off Master's other sock and I went to work on the coals. Master said, "Poole, help me to get undressed. I fear I shall spend a few days gazing at my footboard." Mr. Poole said, "Very good, sir," as he always does and got Master to stand on his one foot, then he helped him to the end of the bed where Master could hold on to the footboard. Usually Master uses his dressing room, of course, but no one could think of his making extra steps. As I had my back to them, bent over the fire which was taking some work to get up, being cold these two days, they paid me no mind. I could hear the rustle of Master's shirt coming off, the clink of his studs and cuffs, and he gave a little moan, I thought when he put weight on his bad foot to help Mr. Poole get his trousers off.

When I stood up and turned around, Master was sitting on his bed in his dressing gown, looking like a sick boy but for his silver hair. He eased himself back among the pillows and spoke to us very weakly. "Poole," he said, "stay with me a few moments. I have some errands that must be done at once and I shall trust them only to you." Mr. Poole was at arranging the pillows and I could not see his face but I had no doubt it was very smug, for he likes nothing better than to be singled out by Master. "Bradshaw can mind the hall while you are out," Master went on. "Mary," he said, turning to me as I was going out, "have Cook send me something. Some tea. Broth, if she has any. I could eat that. Tell her I have no appetite. She'll know what to do."

"Yes, sir," I said and went down. I thought, good, I could clean myself up while Cook got Master's tray together and so be more presentable, for I hate Master to see me covered in coal and I'm afraid to touch anything until I can get a good scrubbing. In the kitchen Cook had a big kettle going already, so I poured some of it in the basin and washed my face and neck, my hands to the elbows. Mr. Poole came through in an agitated state, saying he might be back for tea or not, as Master's errands would send him to the corners of the earth. Then he was off and Cook and I was very companionable for a bit, getting Master's tray together. "He needs a bit of meat," Cook said, "and I've such a nice bit of pork, but there's no point sending it as he'll never get it down."

"He looks very weak," I said.

"And so he must be," Cook replied. "I thought this assistant was to save his health, but it seems he only makes him worse." I did the toast and Cook had some eggs cooked soft as Master likes them, turned out of their shells into a bowl, also some beef broth, a bowl of wild strawberries and a pitcher of cream which, she said, "He mayn't eat, but they might tempt him. They are his favourites and so hard to come by," and a pot of tea. We put no flower on it as it was the bed tray. I put on my best cuffs, which I like to use when I am waiting on Master, and went up with the tray, which, with the white linen and bright-flowered dishes made a lovely sight, I thought, and must lift Master's spirits to see it.

I tapped at the door with my foot, as my hands was not free, and Master called out, "Come in," so I pushed the door open feeling now everything is right again.

Master was sunk in his pillows but his eyes was open and he smiled at me saying, "Ah, Mary. Here you are." I brought the tray around the bed and set it across him while he helped a bit, pulling himself up and setting the legs in place so it would be steady. "I'm so cold," he said. "Please bring me the lap robe."

It was a wonder to me for the room was that close I felt I could scarce find my breath, but I did as Master bid me and slipped the blanket up under the tray so that he was covered down to his feet. He watched me, seeming dazed. "Should you be doing something for your poor ankle, sir?" I said, for I was arranging the blanket so that it would not rest too heavily on his foot. "Perhaps a soak in hot water?"

"No, Mary," he said, so weak-sounding that I looked up to see he'd dropped his head back into the pillows and closed his eyes.

"Should I pour your tea, sir?" I said.

"Please," was all he said and that without opening his eyes.

It was awkward to bend over him and pour the tea but I did it, then stood back for him to take up the cup. He looked at me as if he understood what to do but could not do it. "My hands," he said.

"What is it, sir?" I said. "What am I to do?" He lifted one hand to me, speaking all the while. "I've no feeling in my hands, Mary. They are so cold." So I took his hand in my own and felt a shudder, for it was like taking up a block of ice. "Lord, sir," I said, and chafed his hand in my own as best I could. I did one, then the other, and he seemed to revive a little. "We must get some heat into you," I said. Master raised himself on the pillow then and I brought the teacup to his lips. He took a swallow, then another. "Very good," he said. "This is what I need."

So I got one cup of tea down him, then I broke up the toast and stirred it into the eggs and fed him a bit of that. I told him to put his hands around the teapot, which he did, getting warmth from that, and I spooned some of the hot broth up for him as well. He took everything very grateful and seemed to want to do as I said. After a bit he took the spoon from me and finished up the broth, while I stood by waiting to see what I could do. He was slow, moving most careful as if it hurt him to lift the spoon, and he did not speak except to sigh as he set the spoon on the tray and said, "That's enough."

"Won't you try your strawberries, sir?" I said. "Cook said they was your favourites."

"No," he said. "Ask her to save them for me. I have one matter to finish and then I must sleep."

"Yes, sir," I said, and took up the tray.

"When you're done with that, Mary," he said, "I want you to bring me my cheque-book from the drawing room. I believe I may have left it out on the desk."

This gave me a jolt, as if Master's cold hand had closed around my heart, but I didn't let it show on my face. I said, "I found it out when I went in this morning, sir, so I put it away." Then I felt we was both of us thinking that we both knew *he* hadn't left the book out, as he wasn't in the house to do it. So he seemed to me a little nervous when he said, "Yes, well bring it here, as I can't go there. I believe I made an entry that is not complete."

I felt a great confusion, as a buzzing in my head, and I knew part of it was sadness that Master should lie to me and I to him, but I couldn't bring myself to say I had gone down in the night. So I stood holding the tray, frozen there, and I looked at Master with all my feelings in my face. His eyes met mine, but only an instant, for the lie stood between us and he could not look at me. I turned away and took the tray down to the kitchen where Cook poked into each dish to see what was eaten. "He's so weak I had to feed him with a spoon," I said, and Cook shook her head over it all, saying, "This is the worst he has ever been."

I went to the drawing room, took out the cheque-book and filled the pen. There was the ink spot on the blotter to remind me that I had not been dreaming; it was not Master who used this book last. But, I thought,

Mr. Edward Hyde might write as much as he liked, Master's cheque was no good without his signature, so perhaps that was what Master meant when he said he'd made an entry that was not complete. It made my hands tremble; I longed to open the book and see for myself what was there, but I hadn't the nerve. I could have done it last night, but then I hadn't the wits.

A sound at the window startled me—a pigeon, I saw at once, flying up to the eaves. Then I felt a movement behind and turned to see it was my own reflection in the bull's-eye glass over the desk. "You're as nervous as a cat," I said to myself. It seemed the room glowered and listened to me, and that a shadow was over everything so I could not see. The big vase of roses, the little statue of a man holding up a ball, the green-and-gold angel in the fanlight over the window, all the things I usually find so friendly and comforting seemed to brood upon me and wish me ill. I hurried away, clutching the leather book that, I told myself, was really none of my concern, and ran up the stairs to Master's room. I tapped at the door, received no answer and pushed it open slowly, for Master had bid me come back, to find him—asleep. He lay flat on his back with his hands folded over the lap robe, his bare feet sticking out at the end. I crept in a little, not certain what to do, but then, as I could see he was sleeping very sound and it would be a pity to wake him, I made up my mind to cross the carpet quietly and leave the book on his bedside table where he would find it when he awoke.

So I did and could not leave without taking a long look at my sleeping Master, for he was much altered and in such a way as to touch my heart. His mouth was open, and though he did not snore, his breath seemed to come and go with a catch at the throat. Awake, Master's face is filled with intelligence and kindness, but asleep he seemed to me melancholy, his brow furrowed with some private worry, though perhaps this was only my fancy. It shocked me to see too that he looks old, though the bones in his face are so sharp and elegant, age only makes him the more distinguished and respectable-looking. One lock of silver hair had strayed over his brow and it was all I could do to keep from pushing it back, wanting to arrange him, I thought, as if he was dead.

Then, at the thought of Master gone forever, my heart grew heavy and I turned away. If he keeps on as he has, I thought, that day may come too soon for me to bear.

*M*aster is on his feet but it has been a struggle for us all. For a few days he was too sick to do much but sleep, then for another day he was patient, for he knows as well as any the danger of thinking he must be well because he has tired of being ill. Cook and I kept ourselves busy thinking of ways to make him feel he has no need to be up and about, Cook sending up little dishes to eat at all hours to tempt his appetite, and indeed she had great success, for even in his blackest mood Master brightens at a custard or a plate of toast with marmalade, and I by changing things about in his room, bringing fresh flowers, some coming from our own garden, trying to keep the room aired (though Master do have a horror of an open window and a cold grate) and running about the house for books, papers or journals. Mr. Bradshaw, who is so clever with things, come up with a way to adjust Master's bed tray so that it tilts and makes a writing table, which pleased Master, for he has a great correspondence, fallen behind of late, and so he could attend to his good works without leaving his bed.

But of course after a week his patience was worn thin and he would be up hobbling about, though mindful of his ankle this time so he would ring or call out to be helped up and down the stairs. He received a few guests, Mr. Utterson and Mr. Littleton, who only makes Master angry so I do not like to see him come in, and Mr. Zeal, his wine merchant, who makes Mr. Bradshaw amused by his name and manner, which he says is all one, and so we mun hear about the zeal of Mr. Zeal and how all his customers has zeal for Mr. Zeal, which makes poor Annie laugh until she is near sick. Then Master spent two long days and into the nights in his library, trimming the lamps down to nothing, and I knew that he would soon be back in his laboratory. His ankle at least is healed and he seems to walk upon it with ease and there is some colour to his face. This morning, just as I expected, he took his breakfast early in the library and by ten, as I was hanging out the table linen in the yard, I saw him come out the kitchen door and stroll across to his laboratory, looking cheerful, for it was a gorgeous morning, with a nip of autumn in the air but the sun pouring down from a blue sky, such a day as we rarely see, which was why I had done as much washing as I could find. He stopped at our garden and looked over it smiling. Then I came out from behind a cloth and wished him a good morning. He greeted me, saying it was a fine morning and what a wonder our garden was to see on such a day and how it had altered the whole aspect of the yard, which had once been so dingy he would never have thought to pause in it.

I thanked him, thinking he would go on, but he bid me come and talk to him on the subject of our plants. I left my cloth in the basket and crossed over to stand beside him. "I don't know the names of all these flowers," he said, "though I know that is digitalis, for its use as a medicine." He pointed to the foxglove, which is the tallest of our plants.

"I only know the common names, sir," I said. "That's foxglove to me. And lavender next it. In that circle is lovage, and those tall pink ones is angelica."

"You have laid it all out so pleasantly," he said.

"That was Cook's doing, sir," I said. "I only followed her instructions. She planned it after a garden she saw in H_____."

"Ah, she could plan it, Mary," Master said. "But she could not have *planted* it without you. The energy is yours and we all profit by it."

I could think of no response as Master's compliments do always make me come over so shy, and also it is not my place ever to contradict him in this or any matter, so I stood silent looking at the garden and I felt a swelling of pride, for it is truly a pleasure to the eyes and nose of anyone as passes. But when I looked up at Master, I saw his thoughts was already somewhere else, for he was gazing at the door of his laboratory with a look almost of worry, so I thought he has some problem not yet solved and has only stopped at the garden for a distraction. And indeed one hand had already strayed to his pocket for the key, which he drew out and looked upon as if it was a surprise to him to find it there. So I looked on it too and without thinking I made a sound of impatience, just a rush of air through my nose, but in the quiet it seemed very loud, as if I had spoken my feelings about where that key must take him.

"No, Mary," Master said. "My work doesn't have such pleasing results as yours. It may finally be of benefit to no one. It may only make the world more strange than it is already, and more frightening to those who haven't the courage to know the worst."

Still I did not speak, for I could hardly understand what Master might mean, so, as is my habit, I was trying to memorize it to put down later and I think I have got it as he said it. Then he said, "Yet I must do it," closed his fingers over the key, crossed the yard to the theatre and in a moment he had disappeared inside.

*M*r. Poole has seen him.

I went to K——— to get a fish for Cook this afternoon and while I was out he came to the front door. He addressed Mr. Poole very bold and when he was told that Master was not to home, he said he knew it because Master had sent him to the house on purpose to take a book from the library.

Now this made no sense to Mr. Poole, nor does it to me, for Master was at work in his laboratory and if he wanted a book, why wouldn't he have sent his assistant across the yard to the kitchen door? But Mr. Poole said later he thought it was the proper course to send him round the corner, as we might be taken aback to see a stranger come in at the kitchen, and Mr. Poole says he does not doubt that in the future he mayn't come and go in that way. I thought, but he comes and goes that way already, only in the dead of night.

So Mr. Poole thought there was nothing for it but to let him in and he went ahead opening the library door. Mr. Poole told Mr. Bradshaw he thought the errand would only take a moment and so he stood at the door to wait. Mr. Hyde went in and Mr. Poole said he had an air of being too pleased to be in the room and too comfortable, for he looked all about, rubbing his hands together with a kind of glee, then running his fingers over the big medical dictionary that sits out on the stand. He turned to Mr. Poole and said there was no need to attend him, he'd find his own way out. But Mr. Poole didn't like that idea at all, so he stood there as if he hadn't understood. Mr. Hyde looked him up and down until, he told Mr. Bradshaw, he felt his skin begin to crawl, but he stood his ground, even when the man came towards him and, without another word, closed the door in his face.

When Cook told me this I confess it struck me so I laughed and Annie, who was next to me, hung her head forward and said, "Noooo," for we could all of us imagine the look on Mr. Poole's face as he stood there.

Then Mr. Hyde stayed in the room for a quarter of an hour while Mr. Poole paced about in the front hall, being sure Mr. Hyde would not go out without being seen again. At last he appeared, clutching a book to his coat and seeming annoyed to find Mr. Poole waiting on him. He asked if Master had not spoken to the staff about him and Mr. Poole said, yes he had; we all understood that Mr. Hyde was to have perfect liberty in the house. At this Mr. Poole said the little man (for he is very small) laughed and looked about the hall as if looking for something to smash, to show Mr. Poole what liberty meant to him. Mr. Poole told Mr. Bradshaw he has a wolfish way about him and seems to hang his head as if he expects to have blows hail down upon him. "You needn't look after me, then, Poole," he said. "I'm not likely to take anything that isn't mine."

Mr. Poole recovered to his own satisfaction by saying, "I only want to be of what service I can, sir, should you require any assistance," but Mr. Hyde replied, "For the moment the only assistance I require is that you open the door and stand aside, rather than standing between it and my speedy departure," or some such rude remark that shocked Mr. Poole into doing just as he was told, and in a moment Mr. Hyde was out of the house.

I got this all from Cook, who had it from Mr. Bradshaw, who came upon Mr. Poole immediately after Mr. Hyde's departure, when he was in such a state that he dropped his usual caution and poured out the whole story. I asked Cook what else Mr. Poole had said about Master's assistant. She puzzled a minute and put down her spoon, as if she could not stir and recall at once.

"Well," she said, "he says he is very young, that his voice is coarse though he speaks well enough and must have got some education somewhere, and that his clothes is well made, of good quality, even to his boots, which was made by Master's own bootmaker. He is small, and, as I said, has a deal of dark hair, dark eyes, and is clean-shaven." Cook paused and then added, as if to put the finishing touch on her picture of Mr. Edward Hyde, "Mr. Poole said that he may dress and speak as well as he likes, and give orders in this house until his breath runs out, but his beginnings is stamped on his features and no one will ever mistake him for a gentleman."

Then we spoke no more on the subject and Mr. Poole was silent on the matter at tea, nor did any of us have the nerve to question him upon it, though I could feel the name of Mr. Edward Hyde hanging over the table like a cloud. In the evening Master came in at a decent hour and had his dinner in the dining room, joined by his solicitor Mr. Utterson. They sat over their port so late that Mr. Poole come in and bid me go stir up the fire as it had burned very low, and after that he said Annie and I could be off to bed. So I went upstairs. Along the hall I could hear their voices and it seemed to me they was not in agreement. I tapped at the door and Master called out for me to come in. As I did I heard him say, "I'll say no more about it, Gabriel. You must trust me in this matter," and I saw Mr. Utterson shake his head, his lips pressed tight together, as if to shake off what Master had said to him.

"I've come to do the fire, sir," I said. Master gave me a long look that seemed to fasten me in my place and then he said, "That won't be necessary, Mary. Mr. Utterson is just leaving."

Mr. Utterson seemed startled, but only for a moment. Then he was gathering himself up saying, "It's true. It is very late and I must be in Chancery Lane early tomorrow."

So I went out. As I walked along the hall I thought, they was arguing about this Mr. Hyde and Mr. Utterson likes it no more than do we, so perhaps he has met the young man or knows about his situation and is worried for Master's welfare. How I knew this, I can't say, but I think I was right. Then I thought of what Mr. Poole told Mr. Bradshaw, that Master's assistant had his beginnings stamped on his face, and that he is no gentleman.

What is he, then? A young man from Master's school? Has Master taken him on as a sort of experiment, or just out of curiosity? Is he looking into *his* life with the same sympathy and interest he has shown in looking into my own?

The answer to this question come to me quick and it was this: with more interest than that, for he has set Mr. Hyde no limits and taken him as his companion in those long hours when he works in his laboratory towards some frightening end he has told me himself takes all his courage to pursue.

*T*his morning was cold and damp, and the air so full of dust we could hardly breathe. My hands was both of them numb when I woke so I could not move my fingers and the scars in my neck was throbbing so I thought they must be standing out, but when I looked in the hall mirror I saw I look as always. In the kitchen I filled a bowl with hot water and thrust my poor hands in to get some feeling. Cook was muttering over her pots, seeming in an ill humour, but when she saw me soaking my hands she said, "It's in your hands as you feel it Mary, but with me it is my sore old knees," and I said, "I suppose we are in for some bad weather, by the look of us." She said, "You may say so." Then I thought, Cook knows of the trouble with my hands and has surely seen enough of them to notice the scars, but she has never asked how they come to be so. But servants' ways is not to speak on such things, out of courtesy, for no one could imagine that there was anything but bad recollections attached to such hands as these, so why speak of past sadness.

After breakfast I had a deal of coal to get in, for the coalmonger had come, and soon I was as black as the air around me, but feeling good and warm in spite of it, for the shovelling is work such as cannot be done without drawing up some heat. I laid the grates downstairs, then filled a scuttle to carry up to Master's room. Mr. Poole come in to say Master was up and in his library, where he would have his breakfast, so I thought, good, I can go up as I am without him seeing me, which I did. Then I was down, and seeing as Cook was done in the kitchen and off to the market and I was already black from my work, I thought to scrub out the kitchen floor, as the oven was up and it might dry out before she returned. I got my buckets and brushes, tied up my skirts and was hard at it when Mr. Poole come in, looking as vexed as if all his plans had been crossed, and told me Master wanted to speak to me in the drawing room at once. I looked up at him, for I was on my knees and said, "But I can't go in to him like this. I'm black as a nigger and wet to the knees," but Mr. Poole did not care for my difficulty and, saying, "Master won't be kept waiting," turned and walked away.

So I got up, washed my face and hands at the clean bucket, untied my skirts and wrung the water from them, wiped and dried my boots, put on a cap and a clean apron, which only looked foolish, I thought, as my skirt was black underneath, but it was the best I could do, so I went up to the drawing room door and tapped lightly, wishing I could make myself smaller somehow so that Master might not notice me at all.

Master called out, "Come in," sounding impatient, so I opened the door and stepped inside, closing it behind me. He was at his desk, writing away hurriedly, and I saw a cheque lying out beside the sheet of paper on which he was writing. He glanced up only to see it was me and said, "Come in, Mary," very sharp, then turned back to his writing. I felt timid as I knew I had never seen Master in such a state, nor has he ever spoken to me sharply. It seemed the whole room was full of agitation and Master at the centre of it, filling a sheet of paper with angry words, and I knew at once why he had sent for me. It was to carry his anger out of the house.

Still he kept writing, so I made up my mind to be still and wait upon him. He reached out for an envelope, looking up at me again, but only for a moment, as if to make sure of me. His mouth was set and he looked at me so cold, I felt he hardly saw me, that I was some object to him, useful like his pen or his cheque, such as only exist to serve his will. A rush of anger came upon me, but I fought it down, remembering my place and my duty. Why, I thought, should he think of his own hands when he needs them? No more should he think of me.

Master signed the page, folded the cheque inside it and put them both in the envelope. I did not need to look at the name he wrote on the front, for I felt I knew it. Then he turned to me and said, "I must send you on an unpleasant errand this morning, Mary."

"To Mrs. Farraday," I said.

This startled Master. He sat forward a little and seemed to focus his eyes closely upon me, the way birds do when they see something to pluck in the grass. "How do you know?" he asked.

"I don't, sir," I said. "Only I can think of no other errand you might send me upon that might not best be carried out by Mr. Poole."

Master looked as if he might answer, but his eyes fell on the letter in his hands and the sight of it seemed to distress him so that he forgot all other cares but that which it contained. He held it out to me, speaking as he did, "I rely on you entirely in this matter, Mary. Though I cannot tell you the nature of it, I can tell you that it is of such importance to me, of such importance . . ." Here Master fell silent and once again we was both of us looking on a letter I did not want to take. But I put my hand out, as if Master's will was the same as my own and said only, as I tucked the envelope in my sleeve, "What am I to tell Mr. Poole?"

Master looked annoyed. "Why should you have to tell him anything?" he said.

"If I go out now," I replied, "leaving my work undone."

"I'll take care of Poole," Master said. "Set your mind at rest upon that."

"I will, sir," I said, though my mind was not at rest, nor would it be, I knew, for some time to come. "Will there be a reply?"

"Yes," he said. "I don't doubt that there will be."

"Shall I go at once, then, sir?" I said.

Master nodded, his mouth set in such a grim line I felt too timid to speak. I wanted to ask if I might take the time to change my clothes, for I could feel the wet cloth soaking through my stockings, but it seemed a frivolous worry next to whatever had provoked Master to call on me so anxious. I made up my mind to change only my skirt and shoes, which I could do quickly in the kitchen, for I had a muslin skirt, too light for the weather but dry nonetheless, in the pantry, as well as my walking shoes. I gave Master a curtsy, which he barely took in, he was so distracted, and went out across the hall, hoping I should have the good luck not to encounter Mr. Poole, for I had no idea what I would say to him. Nor did I see him. Cook was still out, so I had the kitchen to myself. I changed quickly, put on my bonnet and cloak and went through the area to the front of the house. It was brown with fog out so I could barely make out the square, and that cold I hunched my shoulders up as if I could protect my chest by folding myself around it. I hurried along the side street, past the door that, unbeknownst to passersby, leads to Master's laboratory. The fog was hanging just at my eye level, but it was patchy and through a broken bit of it a beam of sunlight shined on the door, showing it up dingy and unkempt, so dreary it seemed to soak up the light and turn it dull. I could not pause to look at it, though I half expected it to fly open and Mr. Edward Hyde to burst out, a thought which was like a little shove at me so that I hurried along, pulling in my skirts behind me.

The trip across the city was a long one and full of strange sights, for the fog would lift and then settle of a sudden, so there was never any knowing what might appear—a tired face, or a horse's snorting head, or a carriage wheel so close it threw up the mud upon the passersby. I went through a low passage leading into S_____, where I clung as close as I could to the damp, brown wall, for the carriages came through at a vicious clip, making a deafening clatter of wheels and hooves, and the horses was nearly mad from it, so that one could be trampled as easily as seen, nor did I have a doubt that no carriage would stop, though its passengers were carried over a solid floor of broken bodies. Then I crossed the dingy square, past the gin palace and the low eating house, keeping my eyes mostly down to see my way through the fog, and not to see the dirty, mean residents of that street, until I come to the door I knew to be Mrs. Farraday's. As I drew up to it I saw a young woman, a girl really, dressed to show her scant figure as well as her profession, passing out. She did not see me for she was clutching a handkerchief to her face and weeping into it as if her heart was broken. I stepped aside as she passed me, and it made my heart sad to see her, spiritless and beaten-looking, though she had surely been, and not that long ago, a fresh, pretty young maid with only innocent sorrows to wear her down. I felt it was no surprise, however, that such a poor creature should come out of Mrs. Farraday's house and I set my resolve that she should not abuse me or imagine for a moment that my bearing Master's letter meant I would have any dealings with her were it not my duty to my Master, who was, I thought, displeased with her as well. I stepped into the doorway and tapped hard against the wood, but scarcely had I done it when the door flew open and the dreadful woman herself was upon me like a fury, for she recognized me at once and fairly howled at the sight of me, grabbing me by the arm and pulling me inside, across a dark hall and into a little drawing room that was, I saw, even though I could scarce *see* anything for the uproar she was making, well appointed with fine carpets and good furniture, as well as pictures, a room one did not ever expect to find in such a street. "And has he sent his little milk-faced housemaid again," Mrs. Farraday was hissing as I tried to get my wits about me. "If he thinks he can smooth this one over with a letter and a few pounds, he's badly mistaken. He thinks he can buy his way out of anything, your master, and that no one who takes his money has a right to speak out against him, him and his bloody favourite he has set loose among us here like a mad dog." She went on to this effect, in such a state I despaired of saying a word, so I unfastened my sleeve, drawing out Master's letter, which she snatched at, crying, "Here, give it me," and then, turning her back on me, she went to the fireplace and tore the envelope open. I saw she read the cheque first and thrust it into her bodice, seeming, I thought, marvellous calmed by the sight of it. Then she opened out the letter and began to read it. I heard the front door open, footsteps, very light and quick, followed by a tap at the door. Mrs. Farraday only turned her head and said, "What is it?" loud, then the door opened and a young woman peeked in, very like the other I had seen on the street, her eyes ringed in red from crying and a handkerchief clutched ready at hand. "Sorry to disturb you, ma'am," she said. "I come to see—"

But she didn't finish, for Mrs. Farraday cut in sharp, "They've taken her an hour since. There's naught to be seen here," to which the girl responded, "Beg pardon, ma'am," and went out.

So I stood with my hands folded, looking at Mrs. Farraday's stiff back and wild silver hair, which was all disarranged, as though she had not combed it in days. The fire burned low and the room had a chill in it, so I wondered she was not shivering, for she had on the same thin dress, cut low to show off her sallow flesh, both in front and back, that she wore the last time I saw her. It took her some time to read the letter. She made sounds of contempt, even grumbled a word or two, though I could not make out what she said. The house was still, but I could hear the sound of voices and footsteps on the street outside, a sound, I thought, one could never escape, living in such a place, no matter how many carpets was put down or how thick the drapery. At last Mrs. Farraday folded up the letter, returned it to its envelope and turned to me. But she did not speak, only stood looking at me with a strange, angry light in her eyes. "He calls upon the goodwill I bear him of old," she said. "And well he might." She tapped the letter across her palm, but kept her eyes on me. "But *that* Harry Jekyll is a different one from this, who sends his housemaid because he hasn't the courage to come hisself."

There was no reply for me to make to this, only I was left pondering what it might mean, nor did I care for any of the possibilities that came to mind. I stood my ground waiting for her to decide, which she seemed to be doing by looking at me as hard as she could make her eyes look. Then she smiled in an odd way, not from pleasure but from some dark idea that had come to her. "I suppose you know naught of this matter," she said.

"Nor do I," I replied.

"Nor will anyone else, I'll wager. Anyone who might matter, to your master's way of thinking."

I said nothing.

"Come with me," she said. "I have something to send your master by way of a reply." Then she passed me, going out of the room, and I followed her into the dark hall and up the stairs. She stopped at the first door, giving me a hateful look as she stood aside so that she could open it before me. "I haven't had time to do up this room this morning," she said. "You may find it a little awry, not to *your* standards, I'm sure," and with that she threw the door open. I stepped forward, then as I took in the scene before me I froze where I stood.

It was a bedroom. I know now that it was, like the drawing room downstairs, well furnished with such quality as was a surprise in such a place, even to the wallpaper, which was a dark green but most fresh-looking. I took this in without noting it, for all I saw was the twisted sheets and blankets on the bed, which was all soaked in blood, and the stains down the wall, as of fingers dragged along, which had turned almost black on the dark paper but was surely blood, as was the dark, damp patches on the carpet nearby. Also on the carpet was a white night shift, like my own I use for summer, though it could barely be seen to be white for it was soaked in blood, which had dried brown and stiff. It was ripped at the neck and all the lace pulled away and there was also rents in the skirt. Next it was a linen handkerchief in a like condition.

I could not speak but took in my breath and clutched the frame of the door while Mrs. Farraday stood next to me pouring poison into my ear. "It's quite shocking, isn't it my girl," she said. "Such housekeeping as this. I'm sure you've nothing like it in Harry Jekyll's fine house on the square. You see, we need a maidservant here, such as yourself, to help us with the cleaning and making things up, and the fires as well. Look at that grate, as cold as Job's comforters."

I did not move. She went past me into the room. She stood on the carpet near the bed, looking about her as if the dreadful scene was the setting of some theatre piece she mun do her part in. "And the linen," she said. "It's in a shocking condition here for lack of help." She bent down and took up the handkerchief, holding it out towards me, nor could I look away from it, for it seemed to fascinate me. She approached me slow, saying, "Take this, my girl. Take this to Harry Jekyll from Mrs. Farraday." I kept my hands pressed against my skirt but she took one up roughly in her own. I did not resist her but let her press the stiff cloth into my palm. "And tell him all will be as he wants. His precious name is safe. No breath of scandal as will come to his door, though the doings in this house may stink to heaven." I backed away from her, clutching the handkerchief and feeling such a tide of horror I could scarce keep myself from running, for I saw in the corner of the cloth, embroidered in blue thread that now was deep brown with blood, the monogram HJ I knew so well. Mrs. Farraday saw what I saw, and she gave a little snort of laughter. "Give it back to him," she said. "And tell him this is such linen even his old friend Mrs. Farraday cannot clean for him."

I could not move though I wanted naught but to be gone from that hateful place. "What does it mean?" I said, but speaking to myself, as I knew Mrs. Farraday would not give me the answer to my question, even if she knew it. I folded the handkerchief as best I could and thrust it into the pocket of my cloak where I seemed to feel the weight of it pressed against my side. Mrs. Farraday had turned away from me to close the door to the bedroom and when I heard the click of the lock it seemed to release me from my stupor, for I turned at once and went down the stairs to the front door, which I opened, not looking back until I had closed it behind me and stood safe on the street.

Then I couldn't think, I could not let myself think, so I made my way home as fast as ever I could, barely looking right nor left, telling myself only that when I spoke to Master he would make all this darkness light for me.

But when I come in, Cook told me Master had gone out to his solicitor in a great hurry and sent Mr. Poole on a score of errands, and even Mr. Bradshaw had been called on to run off somewhere, so there was no one in the hall, nor had there been all morning and we might have only the three of us, Cook, Annie and myself for tea, which Cook said was just as well to her as she was feeling done in.

As we'd three quarters of an hour to tea, I told Cook I would go up to my room to change and so I sat here to get everything down as I could, for my head is so full of fear for Master I must do whatever I can to stay calm, so that, when this is all made clear to me, I may find the best way to serve him.

I hate to set down what I must now set down. No more can I keep it to myself. I spent this day so low from what passed between Master and me last night that I could scarce do my work. It seems a great weariness like a heaviness has come over me and I am so clumsy from it that when I knocked over a vase of flowers in the drawing room, breaking the vase and the water spilling everywhere, I only stood there looking at it as if I could not think how to set it right. I go over Master's words to me again and again, but it is as if they was not spoken to me in my own language, and so I make no sense of them no matter how often they pass through my head. Indeed, at Mrs. Swit's we had a French girl with us awhile and she would often watch us talking with a knitted brow, straining to make out what we said, for we might be talking of our work or a fire in the next room for all she knew, and that is just how I feel about what Master said to me. I cannot make it out, but I fear it.

Cook, Annie and I had our tea alone yesterday, as Cook thought we might, though near the end Mr. Bradshaw come in and then Mr. Poole, but they just took a cup standing and went off to their duties. As we was cleaning up, Mr. Bradshaw looked in to say Master had come in and ordered up his dinner at the usual time in the dining room. Cook said she'd a bit of sole for him which would not take long to do so I might finish out the kitchen floor as I'd started in the morning and she would do her pantry and shopping lists. I was glad to take up some occupation, for my thoughts was such a jumble, and indeed as I pushed the brushes back and forth I began to calm a bit, thinking of possible explanations for what I saw at Mr. Farraday's. One that come to me was that a babe coming makes a lot of blood, and perhaps Master had only assisted some poor soul into the world, but that did not explain why Mrs. Farraday was so angry, though I thought perhaps the mother had died and Mrs. Farraday blamed Master for it.

After I finished the floor I washed myself, then helped Cook with the 'tatoes and rubbed up some silver Mr. Poole had put out. Mr. Poole took Master's dinner up, then we had our own, none of us with much to say for we was all of us done in from going about town, only Mr. Poole said the fog was so bad he had walked past the chemist's door and didn't know where he was till he saw a carriage right before his nose and realized he'd come to the corner. No one asked me where I'd gone, and it seemed, as we'd *all* been sent out, no surprise that *I* had been sent out, so nothing was said about it. I thought Master would wait a bit to send for me on some household charge, which was just what happened, for after we had cleared up and Cook and I was talking about what work was to be done in the garden now cool weather is upon us, Mr. Poole come in and said Master had sent for me to do up the fire in the drawing room.

So I went to the pantry to put on a clean apron and while I was there I slipped the handkerchief, which I could hardly bear to touch, into my skirt pocket. Then I smoothed my hair back, looking at my face in a tray, and Cook, who saw me primping, said, "Mary, you look well enough, go along," which made me smile and Cook smiled back at me, for really, I thought, she does care for me. I did not want to leave her and the safe kitchen to go up into the cold house and tell Master what I knew he would not want to hear. And how was I to tell him?

But it was my duty and so I went. Master was seated in his chair before the fire. A bottle of claret was on the side table and a glass half filled next it, which glittered in the lamplight, and as I came in he took up the glass and brought it to his lips. He had on his house slippers, I saw at once, and an old smoking jacket Mr. Bradshaw has been trying to get rid of for months now, but Master won't give it up. Somehow the sight of him so comfortable and relaxed, which usually makes me feel content, as if it was myself relaxing after a fine meal, run against me, why I cannot say. "You sent for me, sir?" I said, sounding sharp—my own voice surprised me—and Master looked up but he did not speak. He put his glass down *very* slow, looking at me all the while, leaning forward in his chair and turned a little to take me in. His look was not cold, nor was it warm, but questioning, and I thought, he is worried that he cannot trust me, but it's too late for that.

"The fire first, Mary," he said at last. "And then you shall give me any message you have from Soho."

So I went and knelt down at the grate, which suited me well enough as it gave me a few moments to compose my thoughts and my face. Still, I did not know *what* I was going to say when Master asked for Mrs. Farraday's answer or if I would have the courage to give him the handkerchief, yet I knew I could not keep it one moment longer than I had to. The grate was hot enough to take the new coals quick and so in a moment I was done. I stood up and turned to Master, who had finished his wine in the few moments it had taken me to do the fire and was now pouring another from the bottle.

"You found Mrs. Farraday at home?" Master asked without looking up from his glass.

"I did, sir," I said.

"And you gave her my letter."

"Yes, sir. She read it in front of me."

Master smiled and tasted his wine. It was the smile he often gives me when he is pleased by my way of speaking, though I did not see that I had said anything to merit it.

"And her response?" Master said.

My heart began to pound in my chest, so that I could scarce speak, and it was very odd for it was as if I had been frighted when really I had nothing to fear. I slipped my hand into my pocket and drew out the handkerchief. Master watched my hand with such a quizzical look I felt sorry for him, and when he saw what it was I held out to him his face went white of a sudden. "She sent you this, sir," I said, "by way of reply." Master took the handkerchief and turned it over in his hands, folding the monogram under so he could not see it. Somehow I found my tongue. "She said all will be well, sir," I said, "but that this is such linen even she cannot clean for you."

Master closed his eyes at these words and hid the handkerchief between his hands. I could not tell what he was thinking, but some feeling was surely strong upon him, for he sat clutching the handkerchief, his eyes closed, while his face took on a look of such pain he seemed to struggle not to cry out. So I felt he was mastering his feelings and did not speak or try to comfort him in any way. When he opened his eyes there was tears standing in them. Then he opened his hands and the handkerchief, which had been crushed between them, seemed to leap up at him and I saw the corner with the monogram unfold as if to taunt him. He jumped up so quick it startled me, went to the fireplace and dropped the handkerchief on the coals. I stood looking at his back while he waited for the fire to catch, but it seemed to take a long time, yet Master did not look away. The room was that quiet I felt I could hear it when at last the edge of the cloth curled up in a line of flame and then, all at once, the rest of it went up in a puff of fire and smoke.

"Mrs. Farraday is right, Mary," Master said, going back to his chair. "All will be well. I'll see to that."

I stood looking at the fire for I couldn't seem to take in that the handkerchief was gone so easy and sudden, as it had cost me such trouble, and I felt in the next moment Master would say that I might go back to my work, which I thought I could not do. The question that come to me at Mrs. Farraday's house come again and I said it out loud, though again more to myself, for I felt I knew the answer but had missed it somehow. "What does it mean?" I said.

Nor did Master reply. I know not if he even heard me. When I turned to him he had settled back in his chair, his glass in his hands, his eyes closed, looking peaceful. "Sir?" I said, and Master looked up as if I'd startled him, but then he spoke in much the same way as he does when we talk of the garden or of his school. "A woman of Mrs. Farraday's character," Master said, "seldom has the opportunity to be squarely in the right."

"That would be her own choice," I said.

"Yes, of course. To some extent. Though such choices as she has had to make may have been limited by her circumstances."

Then I said nothing, for it seemed to me a wonder that Master would seek to defend Mrs. Farraday to me. I couldn't think why he would, or how he could.

"To such a person," Master went on, "the sensation of being right carries with it a wealth of indignation, what we sometimes call righteous anger, often out of all proportion to the seriousness of the situation. Dramatic gestures, overstatements, even some confusion about the truth are not uncommon in such a state."

"She was main angry," I said, "sir."

"Yes," Master said, taking up his glass and giving me a searching look. "I don't doubt that she was. Did she say anything else to you?"

I wanted to reply, not what she said, but what she *showed* me! Though I could see the bed, the twisted bloody sheets, the blood-soaked gown and especially the line of bloodstains on the wallpaper which I knew was made by a hand dragging along, all this was before my eyes as I tried to answer Master, yet I could not speak of it. Instead I said, "She said you thought you could buy your way out of anything, sir."

Master smiled at this as if he expected to hear it. "It would be foolish to expect gratitude for charity," Master said. "Those who need it most often despise the hand stretched out to help them."

Then it seemed I truly would cry out, for I couldn't believe Mrs. Farraday was one of Master's charity cases, for she seemed to be doing well enough and to think Master owed her, and not in the way he described, because she needed it so badly, but because she had earned it by protecting his name, and though I hated the thought of how that might be, I could not take this new picture Master made for me and fit it over what I knew. It would not fit. Still, I have been too many years in service to speak out—indeed, I felt I had already been so bold I could hardly look at Master—so I said nothing but stood looking at the carpet while my poor head seemed to buzz with all it was holding in.

"Mary," Master said. "I am sorry to have to send you out as I have, on such errands, to such a place as that house. I cannot go there myself."

I looked up and saw Master was near pleading with me. "I must trust you," he went on, "to do as I ask and to say nothing of it to anyone."

"I shan't speak of it, sir," was all I said.

Then Master gave me a long look, but not as I have so oft enjoyed, full of kindness and interest, but rather anxious, even fearful, and I thought, what is it he fears? That I should speak, or that I should know?

That was all our conversation, not much to be sure, but it has plagued me all this day and I have gone over it until I think I cannot go over it more, but as I can make no sense on it there's nothing to do but try again. I have made up some stories that might explain this part or that, but none that satisfy me. How can Mrs. Farraday be in a position to save Master's name unless *he* has done something to injure it, and what could he have done if he cannot go to that house but must send me in his place? My first thought, that Master may have helped some poor girl in distress, either to have a babe or perhaps to save her life after she made some foolish effort to get rid of one (for this happens often enough in such a place) would mean that Master had gone there, but if he could go to help, why would he not go on the second errand, which was clearly to make sure Mrs. Farraday would keep his secret? And if he did not go, then how did his handkerchief go? And if he helped some person in distress, why would Mrs. Farraday be so angry and send such a message as she did? And how can Master say that Mrs. Farraday is angry because she is in the right and then that she is angry because she don't care to accept charity?

No. I can make no sense on it and feel as if I am stumbling deeper and deeper into a web of lies. If I trust my own senses, and it seems I may as well, whatever happened in that room had naught to do with charity. A hundred times I have called up the marks on the wall, a hand dragged along, smearing blood as it went, and the shudder that went through me, as if I heard a woman scream. The young girls weeping, looking for someone, and Mrs. Farraday saying "they" had just taken her, and also the words that keep ringing in my ears though I have tried not to hear what they say, "him and his bloody favourite he has set loose among us here like a mad dog," all this must go into the accounting as well.

No, I would have to be blind, and I wish I might be, not to see that there is one story as explains all, that Master's assistant—who has such free rein here he comes and goes as he pleases, and if he may help himself to a book or a cheque, then why not a handkerchief—that he has committed some crime and Master has sent me to Mrs. Farraday to plead and to pay, not just to save his own name, but also that of Mr. Edward Hyde.

We have had a quiet week but a busy one and I have been up so early and done so late I have not writ, nor hardly thought. Master had one dinner party as well as a string of visitors in the afternoons, and has been out to his club, coming in with Mr. Utterson to sit and talk before the fire until very late. He has worked in his library a good deal, only going to his laboratory for an hour or so in the mornings after breakfast.

The weather has been cool but fine, so I have taken the chance to air mattresses and take up some of the carpets upstairs for beating. Cook and I have found a little time for the garden. She says it is time to put up some jellies, mint, thyme and rose geranium, which is one she learned at her country house to serve with butter cake. We hung out some oregano and parsley, which does grow with such a will it is constantly to be cut back so it has any shape at all, to dry in the little garden shed. This is the month to plant garlic. Mr. Bradshaw told us a story that the Queen's cook chews a clove of garlic and then breathes over the royal salad, which made our cook shout with laughter.

I have not spoken to Master, though I see him much. He is always with company or has his head in a book or is going in and out. He tells me good day, might ask for this or that or bid me carry a message to Cook or Mr. Poole, but no more, and I feel when he sees me I remind him of the house in Soho, which, it seems, he wants to forget.

As do I. I want to tell him, but how can I? I know he has said all will be well, but how can I believe it when I know that between us, nothing will ever be as it was again.

After dinner last night I went in to get the fire up in the drawing room and as I was working Master come in from his own meal in a great rush it seemed to me, going straight to the decanter on the side table, pouring out a glass and swallowing it down in a gulp before he even spoke to me, when all he said was, "Mary. I didn't see you there."

"I'm just done, sir," I said, getting up. "I won't disturb you."

"Disturb me?" Master said. He took up a book that was lying open across the wide arm of his chair, snapped it closed and set it back where he had found it. "Disturb me at what?" He threw himself down in the chair, rested his forehead against his hand and looked up at me with an expression of challenge, so I saw that he expected an answer to his question, though he did not think I could give a satisfactory one.

"At your studies, sir," I said.

He gave me an odd smile, as if I amused him, but

only as a dog might, by some unexpected trick. "How do you do it, Mary?" he said. "I wish you would tell me the secret."

"How do I do what, sir?"

"Live as you do. Always at your work, day after day, never complaining, but not like so many, not like a dumb animal in harness, but always so quick with an answer, so calm, so observant. I have the feeling you don't miss much, though you say little."

Now it was my turn to smile and I felt my relief must show too, for it seemed here we was back on our old terms as we have not been these two weeks. "You're in an odd mood, sir," I said, "to be thinking on my life."

"But I'm thinking on *my* life, Mary. My routines, my acquaintances," here he tapped the book he had closed, "my dry studies of an evening with a glass of port and a good fire."

"Study is your work," I said, "as cleaning is mine."

"Study is not my work," Master said coldly. "My work is in the laboratory."

"Of course, sir," I said, feeling chided, for Master seemed to know what he wanted me to say so I wondered why he asked. "That is your work as well."

Then Master sat looking at me without speaking, but I did not feel he wanted to go. "Are you ever frightened, Mary?" he said suddenly.

"Of course, sir," I said. "Everyone as is, sooner or later."

"What is it that frightens you?"

I tried to think and of course the first thing that come to mind was standing in the doorway to that room in Soho and how I felt I would run until I dropped to get away, yet I stood there, and truly there was something that held me that was not fear but wanting to set that fear at rest with some explanation, for I thought there must be one. I could not say this to Master, I knew that, so while the picture crossed my mind I said what I could. "All manner of things, sir," I said. "Bad dreams, noises I might hear when no one is about, anything as is sudden, the horses in the street." I stopped, for Master looked annoyed, as if he wanted to brush away my answer.

"Yes, yes," he said.

"Being hurt," I said. "Being locked up, shut away."

"Yes, of course," Master said, but more gently. "You would be afraid of close places." Then he fell silent.

"What is it you mean, sir?" I said, for I felt he was disappointed in me.

He gave me a long look, as if he could read what he wanted to know in my eyes, which made me feel so unsteady I wanted him to stop, yet I did not look away, even as he spoke. "Are you ever afraid of yourself, Mary?" Master said.

The room was silent about us, but for the clock ticking, which seemed to me loud of a sudden. I thought a long time might pass before I answered but Master and I would not know it, for we was both of us waiting to hear what I would say. At first I thought I would say no, for it seemed a strange thing to be afraid of myself, but then I thought he must mean afraid of what I *might* do, or *might* say, rather than what I am and what I see in the mirror. And it was true that when I feel afraid it is what I imagine that frightens me most, which is, in a way, a fear of what is in my own head. So while Master sat looking at me I went over a great deal and at last, almost as a surprise to me, I heard myself say, "Yes."

"Yes," Master repeated after me, seeming pleased almost. "Yes, I thought so."

I did not speak but waited for Master to dismiss me, for I felt his mind was made up and our conversation was ended, which was right, for the next thing he said was, "Tell Mr. Poole he may close up as he pleases, Mary. I'll be in the laboratory until very late. There's no need to wait upon me." And with that he got up and left the room while I stood wondering, if I'd said "No" would Master then have stayed in his drawing room? But I thought that was not likely, for his mind was made up when he come in and he only spoke to me to firm his resolve, which was to be at his work, so that nothing anyone said to him would change his mind, for he was bound to it, that much was clear, no matter how much he might wish it was otherwise.

have seen him.

After Master left me last night I took his message to Mr. Poole. Then I helped Cook do the porridge for morning and went up to bed at ten feeling tired but eager too, to write up my conversation with Master, which I did as careful as I could before I put on my shift and got in with Annie who was fast asleep.

I do not know what time I woke up. At first I thought it must be near morning, as it seemed the room was light, but then I saw it was the moon, which was full and just risen at such a height to pour into our window. So I lay comfortably watching the cool light on the bureau and feeling pleased with my new winter shift which I had put on, that I thought was too dear when I bought it but the shopgirl said it would be worth the bit extra because, though it is very light and soft, it is warm, and I thought she was right. A few minutes passed in this way and I heard the sound of footsteps coming from the court, seeming far away, then the latch turning and the kitchen door opening, a sound I know so well I scarce marked it but to think Master is coming in from his work.

But as soon as I heard the step on the stair, that quick way about it, I knew it was not Master and I thought, of course it is him, though I had hoped we'd heard the last of him. So I lay still listening to him move through the quiet house, down the hall and into the library I thought, where he stopped and I heard nothing.

He is on some errand for Master, I told myself, some book as he needs, so do not bother about it but go back to sleep. Yet I could not stop straining my ear to hear any sound and for such a long time that now it was the quiet unsettled me. A resolve grew in me as well, to get up, go downstairs and see him. If one of Master's servants is free to roam about this house in the dead of night, I thought, then why not another? So at last I got up, took my summer cloak off the peg and wrapping myself in it, slipped out the door. As I was barefoot, I moved along the hall soundlessly and down the stairs. The house was dark, for all the curtains was drawn, so I stopped at the landing to let my eyes grow used to the dark. There was light pouring out in a thick pool from the library, for the door was open. So, I thought, he has lit the big lamp and made himself quite at home, which annoyed me somehow. I moved along quick, not certain what I would say or do, but only that I would *see* him, and put an end to this mystery of a man with no face. I stepped bold into the light and looked into the room.

He had his back to me and did not hear me. He was bent over the writing table, a book open before him and he was writing hurriedly on the pages of it. He is very small, no taller than I. I saw he was well dressed, though plainly, and, as Cook has said, he has a deal of dark, unruly hair which is longer than the fashion. That was all I could observe before he felt me behind him, though I had not moved, and suddenly he whirled around, making a strange snarling sound, and faced me across the carpet. His face was charged with anger and he had raised his fists, as if expecting an attack, but he took me in at once and got control of himself, so that as I stepped back in fear, he came over quite calm and said in a hoarse voice like a whisper, though it seemed loud in my head, "Mary Reilly."

"I beg your pardon, sir," I said. "I heard noises in the house and then, when I came down, I saw the light."

"Then you know who I am," he said, very cool and seeming pleased to have been discovered.

"You are Master's assistant," I said, for I could not bring myself to say his name.

This made him smile and I wished it had not, for there was that in his smile no woman must care to meet, nor man neither, and I felt myself shrink inside my cloak. His cold eyes was all over me as well. He leaned back against the writing table and gestured to the book behind him. "I was just taking some notes for your master," he said, "upon a little project we have underway together."

"I see, sir," I said.

"I find if I don't get these things down as they come to me . . ." Here he paused, then stepped away from the table towards me, while I felt of a sudden all the strength leave my knees. "But see for yourself," he said, holding his arm out to me as if he thought I might join him. "It might interest you."

I took one step backward. "I'm sure I would not understand it, sir," I stammered.

"I think you would, Mary," he said. His voice was

hard and I did not like the way he said my name so familiar, as if he knew all about me. He stood with his arm still raised, to draw me in, I thought, but I knew nothing could make me take a step in his direction. Yet I felt a strange fatigue come over me, as if my blood had chilled, so I could not make up my mind to move. I heard the hall clock ticking and ticking. His eyes was a cold glare, the way a cat can look, with no feelings to be read, so I could scarcely look at him. Then I thought how I must seem—my bare feet, my cloak pulled over my night shift, my hair all loose and uncombed about my face, and I felt my hands was clutched in front of me like a frightened child, but still I could not speak or move. How long did we stand in this way? And did he think I did not move because I could not make up my mind?

That question brought me to myself. I hardly looked at him, though he stood still in the doorway before me, but I bobbed a curtsy and said, "I beg your pardon, sir. I'll leave you to your work," and then I turned away, trying hard to remain calm though I heard his low laugh behind me. I made my way back through the dark hall to the staircase. There I paused and looked back, thinking I could still feel his eyes upon me, but he had gone back into the room.

It seemed I stopped at every step, and with each one my heart grew more heavy. When I got to our room I knew I would not sleep, so I took up the candle and sat down to write and to wait until I heard him go out.

Something is wrong about him. Cook is right. He is twisted somehow, though where I cannot say. Nor can I tell much about his face, though I looked at him, except that his eyes is dark and that cold it is like looking for your reflection in a frozen pool; it seems like glass but what is beneath is that deep and dark, it gives nothing back.

And Mr. Poole is right as well. He is no gentleman, though he may try to pass for one. How can Master not see this?

There, I hear him. He is in the hall and at the stairs. Does he know I will not sleep while he is in this house?

He seems to think he knows all about me. The way he said my name and told me what I will and will not understand, I can't bear it. Did he come in, after all, just to draw me out, to make sure I know that while he has liberty I shall have none?

Now he has gone out. I hear his steps crossing to the laboratory. No doubt he will tell Master, "I've frightened your housemaid," if he speaks of me at all.

While I must speak to no one.

This morning I was up early, but not before Cook, who told me when I went down that Master himself had only just come in, had gone straight to his room and wanted a fire and then a breakfast tray. So

I put on my apron and went up at once. I did not think Master would speak to me of our midnight visitor, but I wished that he would, for I wanted to tell him he was not the only one deprived of sleep. When I passed the mirror in the hall I gave myself a close look and saw my eyes has dark circles under them and my skin looks pinched, which I did not like to see. I knocked at Master's door and he bade me come in. He was sitting in his chair with his long legs stretched out before him, gazing at the cold hearth, listless, it seemed to me, and not much more life in him than I felt in myself. So I went straight to work, only saying, "Good morning, sir," nor did he speak to me. The wind was wrong, for I could not get the fire up and had to go down for paraffin and back up again, but all the while Master did not move a muscle. When at last I was done and got up to leave he said, "Tell Cook a light breakfast, Mary," he said. "And please no kippers."

This made me smile for Cook does always send Master kippers when she thinks he may have an appetite and he hates them, though I think he eats them now and then out of respect for her feelings.

"I will, sir," I said, and went out.

I stopped before going down on the first floor and looked into the library to see had Master's assistant left the book open, but he must have put it on the shelf and I'd no idea which book it was. It did not seem right to me that anyone should write in a book—I've never seen Master do it—so I thought if I had the leisure to look for it I might find it quick enough, but of course I hadn't and likely never would. So I went down to the kitchen and caught Cook just taking a kipper out of the box.

The rest of the day was quiet enough and we was all of us, Master included, busy with our work indoors. In the afternoon it began to rain. The sound of it falling over the house and the darkness seemed to make us all drowsy; indeed, after he finished his letters in the drawing room, Master stretched out on the divan and fell asleep. I saw him as I was passing in the hall. He took his dinner in the dining room and sent Cook his compliments on her savoury, which pleased her, so she said at our dinner how fortunate we was all on such a raw night to have our place safe and secure with such a Master in such a house, and Mr. Poole agreed, telling of some unhappy stories he'd read about in the papers of servants who was cruelly treated, paid very little, poorly lodged and worked almost to death, all over London, it seemed, such that he wondered how they bore it.

But I could hardly listen, still less join in, for I feel so confused by these last days and don't know where I stand, with Master or with my fellows. Days as this one can go by and nights like the last seem not to matter, almost as if they had not happened, yet my heart is uneasy and can take no comfort, not even in my work. I remember as a child how I felt so often, when days and days would go by quiet, when he was gone or had work and so came and went only to eat and sleep, and I would tell myself, now be content while you can and be *good*, and maybe this time it will last. But it never did.

*L*ast night Mr. Poole asked me to stop at the library on my way up to bed and make sure Master had a good fire, for he'd gone in to read just after dinner and looked to be at it a few hours to come. It was after ten, Annie was already gone up, Cook said she was ready to turn in herself and Mr. Bradshaw vowed he was not far behind. I left my cap and apron off and went up, feeling in good spirits, for we'd had a quiet day, tomorrow is my half-day and the weather, though cold, promised fair. I was thinking of Regent's Park, where I like to stroll and sit, though the gardens are not much to see this time of year. At the landing a breeze guttered my candle, then it went out altogether, but I could see well enough to the light in the library, so I went along, holding my candle out before me though it was useless. When I come to the doorway and looked in, there was Master standing over the writing table, his back to me, looking into a book, just in the same way as Mr. Edward Hyde when I found him here, though Master was not writing. Still, it gave me a queer feeling and I said a little loud, "Sir?" at which Master straightened up very sudden and snapped the book shut, as if he had been caught out, but then he turned to me easy enough and said, "Good, Mary. Have you come to breathe a little life into this fire? It's nearly gone, I'm afraid."

"Yes, sir," I said, going in. Master took up the book and returned it to the shelf as I worked. I noted where it went and the colour of the binding, which was red, thinking it must be the book Master's assistant was so anxious I should look into. But I had to turn a bit to be sure of it, for Master was behind me, and when he had put it up he looked back at me so quick he saw I was watching him, so that when I put my mind back on the fire where it belonged I knew my face was glowing as hot and red as the coals. He took down another book and sat with it in the chair facing the fire, but he did not open it, only sat watching me rake out the dead coals. I wondered could he see my hands was shaking.

"Tomorrow is your half-day, isn't it, Mary?" he said.

"Yes, sir," I said. Then he was quiet and I thought only, please do not let him send me on another errand to that house.

"Have you planned what you will do?"

"Only go to Regent's Park, sir," I said. "As I often do."

"You have a friend you will meet there, no doubt?" Master said.

I couldn't think what Master might mean by "a friend," though it struck me he mun mean a sweetheart, which amused me so I laughed. "No, sir," I said. "I don't think I will, unless you mean old Mr. Tott, the gardener, who sometimes talks with me about the roses." Then, as I was done with the fire, I turned to Master, though still on my knees, and found he was looking down at me, seeming serious and worried, as if it made him sad to think of me, which made me uncomfortable so I said, "No, sir. I have no friend."

"And you've no family," he said. "You don't see your mother."

"Not often, sir," I said. "She's out in Shoreditch now. There's not that much time of a half-day. I send her a little money now and again, and a letter on her birthday, but she cannot read so she mun find someone to read it to her."

"I see," Master said.

But I thought of Marm, in her cold little room, and of the way she looked the last time I saw her, which was some months ago, worn down to nothing, an old woman now, though she cannot be old really, and always at the sewing, day and night, for she works by the piece and gets three shillings a week if she's lucky. She put it down only long enough to give me a cup of tea in a poor cracked cup she has, and then back she was at the needle, and I thought, no, Master did not see, and it was just as well. So I only said, getting up off my knees, "I'm done now, sir, if there's nothing else."

"No, Mary," he said. "That will be all."

But when I was half out the door he said, "Mary?" as if he'd just thought of something, so I stepped back into the room. "Sir?" I said.

"I believe my assistant may have given you a bit of a shock the other night."

So he spoke of me.

"Not really, sir," I said. "I think I surprised him more than he did me."

This made Master's eyebrows shoot up, so I saw he did not expect it. "I fear he was rude," Master said then.

"No, sir," I said. "We hardly spoke once I saw who he was."

"I see," Master said, looking at me very close. "It's as well you've met. I take a great interest in that young man."

"Yes, sir," I said.

Then Master nodded, closing that subject, I thought, and I wondered why he even brought it up if that was all he had to say on it. "Good night then, Mary," he said.

"Good night to you, sir," I said and went out. As I walked along the hall it seemed odd to me that Master and I had said good night to each other, for we never have before. I went up to my room, changed into my night shift and sat by the window to brush my hair out, looking out across the housetops and at the treetops such as I can see, and the moon, which was a thin one, and the stars. I could hear the sound of a cab on the stones, and footsteps of some passerby in the court I could not see. I thought on all these strange events of the last days—that awful room in Soho and the bloody handkerchief, the few words I exchanged with Mr. Edward Hyde, who filled me with a kind of sleepy dread, such as I might feel at the beginning of a nightmare when things may go along right enough and make such sense as dreams do make, still, something is not right and I begin to long to wake up, though certain I will not in time.

I can make no sense on it, nor speak to anyone, even Master, it seems, though I feel him close to me all the time and think we have hardly a need to speak as it seems we are walking in this strange dream together.

*04*fter breakfast this morning Master went straight to his laboratory, so I took the opportunity to sweep out the carpets in the drawing room and library. It was work that needed doing, to be sure, but I had it in my head also that I would look into this book Master's assistant felt so free to scribble upon. I made myself do the drawing room first and thought over whether it could be right to pry in this way, for I never have done such a thing before. Still, even as I thought upon it and saw that I had no business to be looking into Master's books, I knew I would look at it. It seemed almost a pleasure to put off doing it, for I think I knew whatever I found would not satisfy me but only make everything more dark and confused than it is already.

And I was right.

I had to move all the furniture about to do the carpet, then, when I was done, shove it all back in place again, which work made me warm. All the time I worked I knew exactly where the red book was and it seemed even when I had my back to it I could feel it there, like a light behind my head. It was on a shelf too high for me to reach, so before I put the green leather chair back in its place I jumped up quick upon it and took down the book. Then I put it on the low table which is away from the door, so if Mr. Poole should pass I might not be standing in his line of view.

I stood for a moment looking at the cover, which is a fine leather one, as all Master's books is well bound, and edged in gold with the title worked in gold on the spine, but it was in Latin so I could make nothing of it. I opened it to the first page where the title was again, and then the next page with a list of the chapters, which it seemed was each on a subject such as "natural law," or "physical properties," only I glanced at them so quick I could not even make out what sort of book it was. Then I fanned the pages and saw at once that several of them was covered over in the margins with writing, which seemed to me, for I've seen it often enough, to be very like Master's own hand, fine and straight so that a great many words can fit in a small space, not like mine which sprawls so across the page. I opened the book to one of these pages, where the writing was that small I had to bend over it to make out the words.

I wish I could say I did not know the meaning of what was written there. Certain they was such words as I have never spoke nor writ myself, though, growing up as I did, I was not spared the unpleasantness of hearing them often enough. It seemed very odd to read such filth as was there, especially written in so fine a hand. I bent over the page as if I needed to read more to soften the shock of it, or to make some sense of anyone using a book in such a foul way and it seemed the words as I read them was very loud in my head, like someone shouting. But then I had a greater shock, for suddenly through the hateful words I was reading I heard a harsh voice, like a whisper, seeming very close to my ear. "Mary Reilly," he said.

I slammed the book closed and turned around, nearly fainting from surprise. He was standing close behind me but he stepped back, as if to give me room, though not far enough to give me liberty, so I could only clutch the table, helpless to escape.

"I thought you would understand it well enough," he said, lifting his chin to the book behind me. Then, as I did not speak, for I could not, he stood looking me up and down with a horrid smirk about his mouth. I tried to look back, though it is hard to face down such eyes as his, which for one thing is never still. After a long moment I found my breath and said, "I beg your pardon, sir."

He gave me a sneer and turned away. "For what?" he said. "Do you think I care what you read?" Then he went to Master's chair near the grate and sat down in it.

I had a moment to recover myself which I did by smoothing my hair and my apron. The chair was turned away from me and all I could see of him was his arm and hand. The back of his hand is covered with black hair, the fingers blunt, so although, like the rest of him, it is small for a man's, still there is something brutish about it. I found I did not like to look at his hand any better than I liked to see the rest of him, yet there was something that seemed to hold me still and make me stare, as a rabbit will stare stunned by a torch light. He seemed to be making himself comfortable in Master's chair, for he picked up a book from the side table, then turned another around to see the title, as if to give himself a choice.

"Will you have a fire, sir?" I said.

He leaned out over the wing of the chair to look at me, which made me shrink against the table. His eyes is so odd, for though he is young, they are not, and there is dark circles beneath them, caused by lack of sleep I've no doubt. "No," he said. "I won't have a fire." His way of speaking is to mock what is said to him, I thought. "But bring me a pot of tea, Mary," he added.

Everything in me wanted to cry out, No, I will not serve you, so strong that I opened my mouth, then closed it again. He was watching me with his eyes narrowed, looking, I thought, as if he knew what was going through my head and was amused by it. I thought of Master's words—I take a great interest in that young man—and it was that made me find my tongue and say, "Yes, sir. Will you have something to eat with it?"

"No," he said.

"Very good, sir," I said and went out.

Mr. Poole was not in the hall so I thought Master's assistant must have come in through the back stairs.

When I got to the kitchen I found I was right for Cook had seen him through the window come across the yard and let himself in "as if this was *his* house," she said. "And he was up the stairs before I could think of a way to warn you."

"Truly," I said, "we shall have to find a way to make the bells ring upstairs. Perhaps Mr. Bradshaw can rig that out for us, he is so clever with his hands," which sent Annie into a fit of giggles, though Cook thought it was no more funny than I did.

"Where is he?" Cook asked.

"In the library," I said, "asking for a pot of tea, by your leave."

So Cook got the tea tray together while I changed my apron and put on clean cuffs, for it seemed I had got to serve it to him as Cook said Mr. Poole was out on an errand for Master. All the way up the stairs I wondered how Master could allow this man to use his books so and why, after reading what was written on those pages, he did not bar the fellow from our house. Indeed what he'd done to the book seemed worse in my mind than whatever happened in that room in Soho, not because I care more for books than for people, but because one didn't expect to find anything but violence and grief in that other place whereas this was done in Master's own house. But it seemed to me also that the sight of Mr. Edward Hyde must be enough to put off any person of sense. What had he to recommend him to Master in the first place? With these thoughts in my head I carried in the tray and set it down on the table.

He had not left the chair but sat there with a book open in his lap. I did not think he was reading it. He kept tapping his finger against the arm of the chair as I poured the tea out. He was nervous, I thought, and not used to sitting so long. I held the cup out to him, which he took awkwardly, seeming not used to such a fine service. He tasted it, though it was so hot I thought it must burn his mouth, then handed the cup back to me saying, "More sugar."

I put in another full spoon of sugar so that it was sweet as treacle and gave it back to him. He held it over his lap by the saucer, as awkward as a schoolboy, though not with anything innocent about him, and taking up the cup by holding it round the top, drank it down in two gulps. Well, I thought, this does make Mr. Poole's case that he is no gentleman, and the thought of how easily this question was settled made me smile.

"Something amuses you, Mary?" he said, setting the empty cup down on the table beside him.

His voice took the smile off my face quick enough and when I looked down at him, for I was standing across the table, I felt a line of ice run up my spine. He was leaning forward in the chair, fixing me with a look of such hatred I took a step back as if I could get clear of it. I looked down quickly and said, "No, sir," but I could still feel his eyes burning a hole through me, nor did he move until at last I felt tears welling up in my eyes and such a sick, weak feeling in my stomach I feared I might fall down. I gathered up my courage to

look at him again and saw that he had taken up the
teacup, which he was turning round in his hands,
though with his cold eyes still fixed on me. I thought,
he's going to throw it at me, but in the next moment I
heard a cracking sound and saw the cup break into
pieces in his hands.

"What a pity," he said, though still he did not
move. I could not take my eyes from his hands, which
he closed over the sharp bits, squeezing his palms together, then when he opened them I saw some of the
shards had cut him and there was spots of blood on the
white bits and more blood coming at the several cuts.
"Accidents will happen," he said, opening his hands
even wider so that the broken pieces fell to the carpet,
making a clinking sound, very soft, but it seemed a great
clatter in my head. I did not know where to look or
what to do. Of course, I wanted to run, but there was
something so sickening in the sight of his bleeding
hands, the harsh whisper of his voice, that I felt myself
come over cold and clammy, the way it is when a fever
breaks. I stood quite still as he got up and took the few
steps that stood between us. When he leaned over the
table, bringing his bleeding hand to my face, I felt an
aching in my chest and a sob broke out from my mouth,
but still I did not pull away. I knew the tears overflowed
but I could not raise my hand even to brush them away.
I closed my eyes when his hand touched my face, just
at the corner of my mouth, and I kept my eyes closed
while he dragged his bleeding fingers slow, slow, across

my mouth, pulling my lips apart. I gritted my teeth and tried to take in a breath of air, for it seemed I was stifling, that the room was full of the smell of blood and the air could not be breathed for the thickness of it. I could hear his low laugh, and then his horrid, whispering voice. "Don't you know who I am, Mary?" he said.

I do not know how I did not faint, but I did not. I was still standing a few moments later, much to my own surprise, when I opened my eyes and found myself alone, with a sound almost of rushing air in my ears and the thick, salt taste of blood in my mouth.

It is hard to write this, feeling as I do, afraid to set down what happened for fear of what comes next. I want to cry out, I will not stand for this, but I've stood for worse, that much is certain, and I've no right to speak now, nor have I ever.

This was a day I looked forward to, because I can go out now, I've finished my work, and I was to walk in the park or look in the shops, with nothing on my mind but the pleasure of having my time to myself. But now I feel I could walk until I drop and no breath of fresh air will come to me, for everything round me is a cloud of lies I cannot find my way through. Nor may I speak to anyone of what I know, what I can make no sense of though I know it, but must carry these things about in my head where they seem to press out all other thoughts. So I write and write in my book, as if I could make the darkness come clear by setting it down on my page.

did make myself go out yesterday, for I could not sit in my room all day, indeed I don't doubt Cook wondered that I stayed in as late as I did. It was cold, though fair, and I walked a long way, paying no mind to where or what I saw, for my head was so full of this strangeness in our house it seemed I took it with me. When I got to the park I sat on a bench and tried to watch the passersby, but they was all in a hurry to be somewhere, or if one or the other might loiter it was with ill intent. I pulled my cloak up close about me and hid my hands in my sleeves for warmth, then I sat, feeling I'd been thrown down on that bench from some high place and must wait to get my bearings before going on.

I began to think on my whole life, of the places I've worked and how I have always tried to do my best and bear my burdens without shirking or complaining, because it has seemed to me there is no other way and, in truth, I am too proud to do otherwise. I know this comes in part from my marm, who was of a like mind, so much that she will take no help from anyone, even from me; though I send her a little now and again, she always begs me not to do it. And I thought of how she is the only family I have, but because of how things fell out I hardly hear of her, nor she of me. When I do see her we don't talk of the past, never of my father, though there's many a scene comes to my mind of her suffering and my own, nor do I wonder why, once he was gone, Marm never went with another man. I know she is pleased that I take care of myself, have had a good character at every place I've been, and I think she feels it a great wonder that I can write, for she keeps my letters; though she cannot read them, she looks at them. So I feel I could never make her life harder by saying everything was not right with me.

I thought of the places I've been and the ways of people I've seen there, of Mrs. Swit, who was so kind to me, and of the masters and mistresses I have served, none of them ever seeming to see me, though their eyes was quick enough to notice any work left undone, and of how my fellows always thought me cold or too silent, or not gay enough, for when the talk turned, as it always did, to having a sweetheart or going out of service by way of the altar, I could not enter in with some story or other about my own experience. Once Sarah Jacobs, at K——— Place, persuaded me to go out with her where there was dancing and soldiers about, and she said with a little luck here was where we would find a good time and a husband, and so I believe she did, for after an hour of standing about in the cloud that hangs over me, she was off with two or three fellows, nor did I see her again. So I remembered how I walked back to our room alone that night, counselling myself, Mary, this will never be your way, so best take things as you find them and not have a notion you can be what you are not.

And then of how I come to Master's house and found everything so quiet and suited to me, and his ways so like my own that I felt I'd stepped into a harness that fit me at last, and that I could stay safe from the light ways that I have never understood and be valued rather for what I am. So I was happy truly in my place and it did not seem odd to me but natural that Master should take an interest in me and rely upon me to speak plain or keep silent by turns. And though he is so far above me, it was to me as if we was equal, for we live in much the same way and know each other's habits and though he has friends enough and goes in and out and has his work, I felt he was like me, not touched by the need for something more.

Like me, not touched.

And then, as I was sitting there on the bench with all the world of people coming and going about me and the cold stinging my cheeks, I felt such a sadness come over me, for though I understand why I cannot be like others and look forward to the future, making plans and provisions for a shared life, still it is hard to bear. Tears welled up in my eyes, so I rubbed at them with my fingertips. All I could see then was blackness and I could feel his hand pressing against my mouth and the sickening weakness that rushed over me. I heard my own heart racing in my ears, his laughter, the sob catching at my throat, and then at my lips I found the taste of blood. When I opened my eyes I sensed that he was near me, so I looked hard at the strangers nearby, but none of them was like him. Then I knew he was behind me, yet I was afraid to look. How long did I sit like this? At last I stood up and turned to face the bench. There was a child running alongside his nurse, and a tall man in a top hat; then, far off by the big gate, I thought I saw a little man, like a shadow, disappear into the busy crowd of the street.

*H*ow cruel it strikes me that I have been thinking so of my marm these last few days and feeling I must find a way to get out to see her, though it takes more leisure to make the trip than I can ever call my own these days, and then to learn this day that I shall never see her more.

This afternoon before tea Mr. Poole come into the kitchen where I was laying out the dishes, holding a letter in his hands and giving me such a look, as if I had no business to receive a letter in my life, that I knew it mun be for me. It were a poor document, written on dirty paper and sealed with a bit of candle wax, my name and our house number printed across the front in big letters such as a child makes. I opened it up at once, though I knew what it mun say, and read the few words writ, I could see, with difficulty, both for the sadness of the message and the uneasiness of the writer with pen and paper. It said, *Your misus Reilly passed on these three days. Please to come at once to Mr. James Haffinger, at lodgings to settle affairs. Yours very truly Mr. James Haffinger.*

I read it quick and felt saddened and angry as well, for I knew Mr. Haffinger meant Marm owed him money, otherwise he would not have bothered himself to let me know of it, and also I felt very confused by his message, for I could not tell how long Marm had been gone or what he had done with her and I wanted her to have a proper burial as she had not had a proper life. Mr. Poole gave me his cold-fish look and then Cook, seeing me holding the letter but not reading it, said, "Mary, what is it? Have you had bad news?"

"My marm has passed on," I said.

Then they was both full of sympathy and told me I must sit down for the shock and Cook brought me a cup of tea saying, "My poor girl," and also that she remembered when her own ma had passed on she felt she'd lost her childhood forever, which I thought an odd thing to say, then it struck me she must mean happy memories. I said, "I mun go out to the East End to see to her funeral, but how can I?" and Cook said, "Why, Mr. Poole will speak to Master and you shall go in the morning," so I saw that it was understood I had good cause. "I never had to see to a funeral," I said; "I don't know a thing about it." But Cook said, "You may find that out when you get there. It may already be arranged." Then Mr. Poole said, "Perhaps your mother had a burial society," but I replied, "That's unlikely, sir. She could scarce get enough to stay alive, so she could not lay by to die." Then he looked away and I thought, he is thinking on his own arrangements which, no doubt, is laid out as careful and neat as his cuffs.

"I shall speak to Master after tea," he said.

All the afternoon I could think of nothing but

Marm, who may be left on her mattress until I can come for her, or else turned out into some storage place so that her room can be let at once, and also I thought, now I am an orphan, for I have no one in the world who knows me. My only comfort was the little money I have laid by, which has taken me so long to save, but there's nearly eight pounds, which Cook told me should be enough for a proper funeral, for a coach at least and a good, lined coffin, a proper pall as well as bearers.

After dinner Mr. Poole called me into his parlour and bade me close the door as I come in. "I've spoken to Master," he said. "And you have his leave to go and attend to your mother's funeral tomorrow. You may leave as early as you like."

"Thank you, sir," I said.

"How will you go?" he asked, as if he thought I would take a hansom.

"I can get the omnibus partway, sir. The rest I can walk."

"I shall instruct Cook to leave you something to take for your lunch."

"Thank you, sir," I said. I wondered he was so cordial, though it was just like him to put on a show of proper feeling whether he felt it or no.

"Has your mother other relations to assist you?"

"No, sir," I said. "She had a sister in Holborn but she's passed on these five years. So there is only me."

"I'm sorry for it," Mr. Poole said. "It will be a sad business for you then, on your own."

I looked up at him, thinking it a marvellous thing

that the passing of a woman he would not have spoken to in life should so affect him he would now speak kindly to her only relation. Perhaps he saw that his sympathy did not touch me, for he stiffened and made to turn away. But then he seemed to have a second thought and said, "Cook tells me Master's assistant was in the house while I was away on Tuesday."

"Yes, sir," I said. And I thought, so that's what is on his mind.

"And you attended on him."

"Yes, sir," I said. Then I took pity on him, for he wanted to know all about it, I could see, and not have to drag it out of me, so I went on. "He was in the library and ordered up a pot of tea, which he drunk at once and then went out."

"I see," Mr. Poole said. "Cook told me a cup was broken?"

I wonder I did not turn pale when he said this. I could see the cup coming apart in his hands and feel his eyes on me, oh, as if he was there before me. I knew I could not speak of it, even to someone as might care for me, even to Master himself, so, as it is hard on me to lie, I looked down at the carpet and said, "I dropped it, sir."

Mr. Poole was ready for this. "On the carpet?" he said.

Of course it wouldn't be likely to break on the carpet, I thought. "No, sir," I said. "By the fender. It slipped off the tray."

Mr. Poole said nothing. I continued staring at the

floor as I know the sight of me hanging my head vexes him and I wanted him to send me away at once.

"Very well, Mary," he said after a moment of this. "You may go back to your duties. Master will want a fire in the library this evening."

"Yes, sir," I said and went out.

I finished my beer at the table with Cook and then put on a clean apron and went up to the library. Master was still in the dining room so I thought I could get the fire up and be off without seeing him, which strange to say I felt best, for I feared he would speak to me of Marm and I did not want to talk about her. But just as I was finishing he came in and took his chair behind me. It was raining out. Even with the curtains drawn I could hear the tapping of the rain against the windowpanes, so I thought it must be raining hard and I would have to make my journey east through no end of mud and filth. I raked out the coals slow then, feeling now I did not want to finish, though the heat was such as made my cheeks like flames. I heard Master take up his decanter and the sound of the port pouring into his glass, but he said nothing. I wiped my hands on my apron, then touched them to my face. I felt I could not move.

"Mary?" Master said.

I turned to him, still on my knees. "Sir," I said.

He was looking down at me over his glass. "Are you unwell?"

I got to my feet. "No, sir," I said. "I'm well enough, only the heat made me dizzy for a moment."

He sat gazing at me, his face full of concern, but he did not speak.

"I'm finished here, sir," I said. "Will there be anything else?"

"I was sorry to hear from Poole of your mother's passing, Mary," he said. "You must take as much time as you need to settle her affairs."

"Thank you, sir," I said.

"Had she been ill?" he asked.

"That is what I don't know, sir, though I will find it out soon enough when I get there. The note sent was from her landlord and he only said she was gone."

"You have no other family to help you?"

"No, sir," I said. Then I thought, my father is somewhere, but I've the good fortune not to know where, and as I had this thought I felt Master was thinking the same thing, for he looked as if something pained him of a sudden. He passed his hand across his eyes and when he took it away I saw there was drops of moisture on his forehead. He gave me such a searching look it was all I could do to keep from reaching out to him, then he said, "You weren't afraid of him?"

"Afraid of whom, sir?" I said.

But Master looked away from me and had fixed his eyes on his own hand, which clutched the arm of the chair with such force as made his knuckles white.

"Sir," I said, for he seemed not to know I was there.

Still he stared at his hand and now his whole brow

was deep furrowed and I saw he had clenched his jaw. It disturbed me to see him so, yet I could do nothing but wait, which I did for what seemed the longest time, then he recovered himself somehow and turned his face towards me. "What did you say?" he asked.

But I did not speak, only gave him a wondering look, which made him impatient so I wished I had been able to say something. "That will be all for now, Mary," he said. It was as if we had not been talking. "Tell Poole I will be late in my laboratory tonight. He needn't wait for me."

"Yes, sir," I said. Then I curtsyed to go out and Master, seeming completely relaxed now, said, "Good luck on your sad journey tomorrow, Mary."

"Thank you, sir," I said and went out, more troubled by the memory of our conversation than by the prospect of my trip to the East End on the morrow.

I was up before dawn and dressed by candlelight in our room. I put on black stockings and my stiff walking boots and pinned my skirts up as best I could to keep them off the ground. I thought it might look unseemly to have them up so high, but I'd rather shock my fellows with the sight of my ankles than drag about in mud all the long day ahead of me. I put on my black shawl, pinned with an ebony brooch Mrs. Swit gave me which I seldom wear, and my dark grey bonnet, as I haven't a black one. Then I went down to the kitchen as quiet as I could so as not to wake Mr. Bradshaw, who sleeps under the stairs.

Cook had wrapped up a piece of mutton and another of cheese, also a bit of brown bread, first in cheesecloth and then in paper tied round with a string, which she put out for me last night, so after I put on my cloak I took up my lunch and went out the area to the front.

It was damp but not raining, and the air was chilly. The gas lamps was still lit though they could scarce do more than glimmer in the fog, which was thick, brown in patches then white in others and shifting about, for there was a breeze. I could hear birds rustling in the square, it was that still, and my footsteps seemed to echo out on the walk. When I come round the corner I heard another footstep, far off at first, but then all at once very close, coming towards me from the corner and at a good clip. I stopped, for there was something I did not like about being in the path of such a rush as this, and I stepped aside against the wall, just at the corner. In the next moment he was passing by me, seeming very close, so that I heard his harsh breath and felt all the air rush about, and I saw him, though not entirely, for the fog was between us. He did not see me, or if he did he did not care, for he was running hard, his head down in his coat like a man pursued, and I knew at once that he was going to let himself in at the laboratory door. I listened as the footsteps came to a halt, then I heard the door open and through the gloom I could just make out a darker bit of fog, which was him, no doubt, going in.

What is he running from? I thought. And does Master know about it? I listened for a moment to hear if anyone was following, but there was nothing, so I went on my way, feeling that to begin the day with the sight of such a wretched creature was surely no good omen.

My way lay across the town, and as I went along the quiet streets come to life before me. The costermongers, coming in from the markets where they had been at their business while I was still in my bed, appeared on every corner, setting up barrows and speaking to one another their rough language, one eye to the street children as will steal from them and the other to the sky as will rain upon them. They paid me little mind, though they sang out their wares to me as to everyone. I went a long way without stopping, then bought an apple off a man who told me it should bring colour to my pale cheeks. He was so gay, so pleased with his fruit—which to hear him talk was all one ever needed to be healthy as well as happy—and, it seemed to me, pleased with his life, though I knew it could not be an easy one, he made me smile. When he asked why I was out so early on such a fine, promising day as this, I hadn't the heart to tell him the sad nature of my business, so I said I was on an errand for my master. As I walked away I thought what makes a day fine for one does nothing for another, so this man and I look out into the same dim gloom and where he sees hope I see naught but difficulty. It has been the bane of my life that I cannot be light at heart as my fellows are.

So I went along, while the streets grew more and more busy, and soon every crossing was a danger to my skirts as well as my life, for the mud was deep in places and once in it, it was hard to step quickly. The horses' hooves make a different sound—not crisp but sucking, though they seem not slowed down by it as we are. I went a way on the tram but might have walked for the time it saved me, for a horse was down, the cab turned over as well, and a dreadful noise of people screaming, mud and fists flying and the poor beast struggling to get to his feet while his driver cut the harness as best he could to free up the cab, so the roadway was blocked for some time.

When I got to the street in Shoreditch where my mother had her lodging, the sun, or the bright patch of fog that might well be all we would know of the sun for the day, was well up over the housetops. The way to her door is a dim alley, the walls slippery with slime, the footway with mud, a drain down the centre that is clogged more often than not, so there is sometimes a narrow river of filth to inspire the passerby with hopelessness. I stayed as close to the wall as my horror of touching it would allow, and stepped across the doorstones of three dwellings before I came to hers. When I knocked there was a shout, a man's voice, then a pause, a clatter like pots falling from the cupboard, then the door opened and a little pop-eyed man stuck his face out at me. "Can't you give a man no peace!" he said.

"I'm sorry to disturb you, sir," I said. "I am Mary Reilly."

The man looked me up and down, sticking his chin at me as he would poke me with it. "That may be, miss," he said, "and very fine for you I've no doubt, but what should it mean to me that I should be summoned to my door to hear about it?"

By the time he'd got to the end of this greeting, I'd drawn his letter from my cloak, which I held out before me. When he stopped speaking, for it seemed he could not talk and look at once, he took in the envelope, recognized the begrimed writing for his own and changed his tone entire.

"Oh," he said, serious as a church. "You are the bereaved."

It was hard not to be amused at his manner, which was so much a show he seemed to make himself up as he went along, but I was tired from my walk and suddenly dropped very low at the thought of where this fellow had contrived to lay my marm, that I took him at his word and leaned against the doorway. "I've come a long way," I said. "And I've come as fast as I could."

"Oh my," he said. "And I've no doubt you have, poor bereaved soul that you are. Come in, come in and sit and I will tell you of your poor ma's passing."

So I went in and he told me Marm had taken ill

early in the month but would not be taken to hospital and kept at her sewing, though she could do less each day, nor would have anyone do aught for her, nor send to me. She passed on in the night, but that morning she had told her landlord, Mr. Haffinger, that should she expire he was to write to me and that the address could be found on the pack of letters in the tin next the tea tin. Mr. Haffinger said that as soon as he knew Marm was gone, for he visited her each day, he got the letters, then it was a day spent getting together a proper bit of paper and another in composing, so he thought I should have got the letter in three days of her going. As he told me this he fussed among the tea things he had on a dirty little stove in the corner of his room and when he turned around he had a cup of tea for me which I took gratefully.

"Is she still in her room?" I asked.

"No," he said, very slow and shaking his head. "That she is not. I've always a great demand, as you may say, for me rooms. I've a little space below stairs which I do not let, but it is safe and dry, and there I have laid her until you should come."

"And her things?"

He gave me a long, sad look, so that I knew I should never see anything belonging to my marm again. "Your poor ma wasn't able to pay her rent the last week, for she weren't strong enough to work, so as it was owing, I took the liberty to clear out her debt by selling off the few bits of furniture and crockery as she had, you know. I'm sure it were not much." He went back to his stove and rummaged in a tin there as he spoke. "But I drove a hard bargain, miss, you may be sure, and in the end settled all your ma had owing and"—he produced a coin which he brought to me—"a shilling over."

I took the coin and sat looking at it in my palm.

"I thought to save it for you, as you might apply it for her interment expenses."

I could not speak. The shilling seemed to weigh in my hand with all the weight of Marm's unhappy life. I closed my fingers around it and slipped it into my skirt pocket. "May I see my mother, Mr. Haffinger," I said, to which he replied, "Of course, of course, perfectly right. Please to follow me." Taking up a candle and muttering to himself all the way, he led me down a dim hall to a staircase that looked as if it would take us straight to hell, it was that black. At the bottom of it was a low-ceilinged hole, with a few inches of black water standing in it and the sound of dripping continual. I heard the scurrying of some animal feet as we went down, but I could see nothing. To my relief he stopped halfway down and turned to a bolted door that gave off the staircase. It opened out on creaking hinges like an oven door and indeed it was not much larger. The space behind it was no bigger than our kitchen table. The floor was dirt and, as he had promised, dry. There was a low pallet and lying on it the remains of my poor Marm. There was no going in to stand beside her, for the space would not allow it. I saw he had slid the pallet in feet first and I felt a rush of relief that he had not taken and sold her shift, which was the only one she had and which she was wearing, no doubt, when she died. Mr. Haffinger held the candle up high so I could see her face, which was near the door. Someone had closed her eyes and folded her hands upon her chest. Her mouth had dropped open so that she had a startled look about her.

"Your poor ma," Mr. Haffinger was saying. "Struck down in the prime of her life." I touched her cheek, thinking to close her mouth, for I did not like the way it looked, but found her skin as cold and hard as a slab of marble, so I drew my hand away, and it was then I understood that she was gone. I backed away from the door and Mr. Haffinger closed it up behind me.

"Now," he said, "you may count upon the parish to see to her burial. She had set nothing by for a funeral, so she told me, but the church here does a fair enough job, so you may say, as I know from my previous tenants what has passed away. I always make it a point to see them to their final rest."

Yes, I thought, your tenants must pass on regular in such a pest hole as this. But I said naught of my feelings. Instead I told him I had some money laid by and wanted Marm to have a proper funeral, at least a coach and a lined box proper, which set him in a whirl of excitement till I thought he would pound me on the back for glee. Of course he knew the only funerary furnishers to see, and vowed to accompany me so that no one might take advantage of my grief, for he said, "These fellows may see a young, innocent, gentle creature like yourself and think they may screw up the price and no one will be the wiser." For, he pointed out, "Your poor ma is not likely to complain."

So I was forced to go out into the streets with this unpleasant fellow who clearly had naught to do and looked upon my marm's passing as a high entertainment. The gentlemen at the funerary furnishers were not much better than Mr. Haffinger, full of fake sympathy and comfort only an idiot would fail to see was a sham from start to finish. They produced a book for me to look at giving the price entire and a description of what they provided, everything from coach to mourning bands, even to the material of the pall, silk being more than velvet, as well as the number of brass fixings on the box. It was all arranged to make my head spin and lay out every penny I had, but remembering both Marm's pride and her dislike of waste and pompery, I kept my head. I had hoped all the business could be concluded in the afternoon, it was for that I left so early, but Mr. Haffinger and the undertaker howled at the thought and said it could not be done before two days, for the parish only buried on Thursdays and the bearers must be engaged a day ahead of time. So I saw I should have to ask for another day off, though I might leave Master's as late as ten and make it there and back by dinner, for the funeral man assured me it would not take above two hours. I paid them half the money, three guineas, and agreed to bring the rest on Thursday. Then Mr. Haffinger would accompany me to the church to engage the vicar, who was a slow-witted fellow I think and, like Mr. Haffinger, carried away by the idea that it should be a proper funeral and that there would be in his audience one sober, sincere, unpaid mourner for the departed one.

So I had concluded such arrangements as I could make by noon and set out on my trip back home feeling heavy-hearted, that Marm must lie three more days in Mr. Haffinger's basement and that I must ask leave and make the long trip back again before I should have purchased a peaceful rest for my marm. I stopped along the way in Russell Square and bought a cup of milk from a man there, as I had a great thirst, then I sat on a bench and ate the lunch Cook had made for me, of which I left no crumb, for I found I had a great appetite, from walking, no doubt, and from biting back so many of the thoughts that rose to my tongue.

When I was done I went on my way as quick as I could. The wind was whipping cruelly at every corner, the streets was crowded and the noise terrific, the vendors all calling their wares, and the clatter of the carriages never ending. There were great crushes of folk around the news vendors all along the way and though I could not read their broadsheets it was easy enough to know what they said, for it seemed at every corner they was shouting out the same story, that an MP was beaten to death on the streets last night and the murderer was still at large.

*W*hen I got in, our house was in an up-
roar. To my surprise it was for the murdered MP I heard
of on the streets, who was, it turns out, Sir Danvers
Carew, a schoolmate of Master's, though not I think a
close friend these last years. I never saw him in this
house, at least. But Mr. Utterson had come straight from
the morgue, where he had been summoned to identify
the poor man, and gone to Master in his cabinet to tell
him the news. Cook said no sooner had he left than Mr.
Poole was sent for and he found Master pale and weak,
his eyes red from tears and asking for his tea to be
served where he was, for he said he hadn't the strength
to come into the house. "He is badly took by this hei-
nous murder," Mr. Poole told Cook, but when I heard
it I thought, why should he be so moved? Everyone
seemed pleased I was back early from my sad errand,
but only Cook asked me the cause of it and when I said
I would have to go again on Thursday, she pressed her
lips together as if it were an annoyance and said, "Well,
Mr. Poole will have to ask Master leave."

So I went into the pantry to take off my bonnet
and put on my apron. I had such mean thoughts then,
it seemed I hardly knew myself, for I thought, this Sir
Danvers Carew was an elderly man who had a fine,
long life with the world to serve him, yet we must make
more show of his passing than my poor marm's, who
was surely too young to die and had never had a moment's rest while she lived, which no doubt accounts

for her giving up and going off so soon. But then I thought of the elderly gentleman being beaten on the street, for the story is he was found so battered about the head he could scarce be recognized, and it seemed a great pity and a senseless thing as well, for Cook says his money was found upon him, so it was not for that he was murdered.

Master came into the house after tea but I did not see him, for I was at work upstairs turning the mattresses which I found was a sewing job in Master's room, for there was a tear in the cover and the feathers was all coming out, so I had to stop and repair it at once. When I come downstairs for the needle and thread, I heard the front bell ring and as I come back through the hall I saw there was two constables following Mr. Poole, whose face was as grey as ash and stiff as a poker, into Master's drawing room. I wanted to go behind and say, What does it all mean? yet I do not like to ask Mr. Poole anything, so I thought I will just finish this job and by the time I am done Cook will have it all and be eager to tell me as well.

Which was just how it happened. When I had the beds made up again, I went down to the kitchen to take back the sewing things and as soon as I opened the door, Cook called out, "Mary, come in at once. This is a dreadful business and I hardly know what to think. Can you believe it, the police is quite positive Sir Danvers Carew was murdered by our master's assistant, Mr. Edward Hyde."

What a confusion of feelings I had upon hearing

this! My first thought was that when I went out this morning and he nearly run me down, he was coming from this murder, that he went straight to Master, and so Master knew before anyone, and that was why he was so taken. Another thought was an odd one. It was that this mun be the last we would see of the fellow, for now he mun run for his own life as there would be no place in all of England where he might show his face. But then, I wondered, how could the police be so certain, which I asked Cook, and she replied, "Why, the crime was overlooked. The underhousemaid at Mister Littleton's house saw the whole thing from her window and she recognized the dreadful man, as who would not who ever saw him once, because he had visited her master. Then the police come up with his address somehow and went straight to his house in Soho where they found a broken piece of the weapon. But here is the worst of it, Mary, it was our master's own walking stick they found there and Edward Hyde had used it to do the deed, and that is what sent the constables to our door."

Then Mr. Poole come in, looking as if he'd just swallowed some unpleasant medicine, and leaned his back against the kitchen door. He looked at Cook, then at me, and Cook said, "I've told Mary what the police has come upon." Mr. Poole flinched at the word "police" and said, "I did not think I should live to announce officers of the law into the drawing room of this house."

"Have they gone?" Cook said.

"They have," he replied. "And I hope they may have no cause to return."

Cook agreed, then Mr. Poole said to me, "Mary, go up to the drawing room at once and see to the fire."

I hardly need say how anxious I was to get to Master. I was out the door and up the stairs at once. The drawing-room door was open and I saw Master's hand on the arm of the chair drawn up before the cold grate. I tapped on the doorframe and went directly in.

"Mary," he said when he saw me. "I thought you would not be back yet."

I curtsyed and tried not to stare at his face, which was so altered it shocked me. It was true, he had been weeping. His eyes could hardly open for the swelling around them. He was disarrayed as well—his hair had not been combed, his collar was all undone, and he was sunk so low in his chair he seemed to have been thrown down into it, wrung out by grief.

"I could not finish my business, sir," I said. "And so must go back on Thursday, if I may have leave. I can make it up if I don't take my half-day next week."

"Oh," he said. "That is no matter. Take whatever time you need and think no more about it. I'll speak to Poole."

"Thank you, sir," I said, and I did feel truly grateful. "I'll see to your fire now."

He nodded, then, lifting his hand weakly as if it was useless to him, he fluttered his fingers at the bottle on the table. "Would you pour me a glass of claret first," he said. "I haven't the strength to get up and get it myself."

"Of course, sir," I said. I went to the table, poured

out a full glass and gave it him. He gave me a poor, weak smile as he took it, so that I felt such pity for him I had to turn away. I got to my knees and set to work on the fire, which took some time, as the grate was cold. Outside we could hear a wind whipping round the house, making the shutters groan on their hinges, and the light was fading fast from the room. When I was done I stood up and turned to Master who was, it seemed to me, so sunk in gloom that I said, "Shall I light a lamp for you, sir?"

He looked up at me. "I'm not sure," he said. "I may not want much in the way of light this evening."

I could not think what to say to this, so I stayed as I was while Master took another swallow of wine. "It sounds bitter out there," he said, looking towards the window. "I'm glad you are not out walking in it."

"Yes, sir," I said. "It was coming on as I came in. But perhaps a good storm will blow all this fog away and tomorrow will be bright and clear."

Master nodded, still with his sad smile. "For a while, yes," he said. "But how long before the fog returns?"

I said nothing. It seemed Master saw through my cheerful remark, as I did myself.

"I suppose downstairs is all abuzz with this miserable affair of Sir Danvers Carew," Master said.

Then I felt uncomfortable, but I thought why should Master care what we say? "Not downstairs alone, sir," I said, "but all over the town. They was crying it on every corner as I came along."

Master sighed. "My poor Edward," he said.

I was speechless, though I thought quick enough, isn't it the poor man struck down on the street who is to be pitied? Master seemed to read my thoughts, for he said, "And poor Danvers Carew. He was a harmless old hypocrite. Certainly he never did a thing to provoke such a"—Master's voice broke, then he recovered—"such a merciless fury."

"No, sir," I said, for Master sat looking at me, seeming to plead for some answer. "I'm sure he did not."

This response seemed to give Master some resolve. "I've had a letter from Edward Hyde," he said. "Which I've given to Mr. Utterson for safekeeping. We will not see more of him in this house. He has gone . . . away."

"I see, sir," I said, though I did not see, unless Mr. Edward Hyde sat down and wrote it before Master's eyes in the laboratory. To have Master lie to me made me so uneasy I wanted to leave, so I said quickly, "If that is all, sir?"

"Yes," Master said, then, "no. I think I will have a light, Mary."

While I was lighting the lamp, he finished his claret and when I brought the light to him he waved me away. "No, put it on that table," he said. "I don't think I can read." I went to the table. "And would you pour me another glass of this claret. It is an excellent wine," he said.

I took the glass. As I poured out the wine Master said, "I'm trying to think of something else, Mary," he said. "Some request whereby I may keep you with me a little longer."

"That is all you need say, sir," I said. "I will not go."

"You looked as though you wanted to get away just now," he said.

If he can read my feelings, I thought, I may as well hold nothing back. "I'm sorry for that, sir." I said. "I was uneasy because as I was going out this morning I saw Mr. Edward Hyde coming in at the laboratory door."

Master's eyebrows shot up, but he kept his voice calm. "He did not see you," he said.

"No," I said. "It was the fog, and he was running, sir."

"Yes," Master said. "Running for his life." I said nothing. "It is marvellous, you see, Mary, how he does love his own life."

"So do we all, sir," I said.

Master responded very quick, as if I had contradicted him, "No. Not as he does."

"I see, sir," was all I said.

"Have you told anyone this, Mary?"

"No, sir," I said. "I have not. Only you."

Master looked down into his wine, then took a drink of it, thinking what to say to me, I'd no doubt.

"Of course I had him write the letter," he said, "because I did not want it known he came to me."

"I see, sir," I said, and I did see very well, for not to have called the constables upon hearing such a tale must surely be a crime in itself.

"I told him I could not help him, Mary," he said. "And he understood me very well. He promised to go away, and stay away."

"Then that is just as well, sir," I said.

"Yes," Master said. "I have done all I can for him." Master's eyes filled with tears. He put his glass down and covered his face with his hands. "Forgive me, Mary," he said. "I have had such a lesson."

I stood looking at Master and it seemed his sadness would become my own. I wanted to reach out to him, but could not, to speak, but the only words that come to me mun say what he already knew.

"It was my own folly," he said. He rubbed his eyes with his fingertips, then looked at me again. "But good can come of it."

"I hope so, sir," I said.

"You may rely upon it," Master said. "I will see to that."

He's like a child, I thought, saying, I will, I will. But how can he will a dead man back to life or save a murderer from the gallows? Master was looking to me to reply to his promise, and I said, "I will, sir." Then I thought, now he has *me* saying it, and that made me smile. But when I met Master's eyes the smile was struck from my face, for he was giving me such a cold look I felt I could not deserve it. "Does something amuse you, Mary?" he said, in a husky voice that hardly seemed his own.

"Sir?" I said. Then he did a thing so strange it made my blood seem to chill in my veins, though it was nothing, really. He looked at his hand, which he had rested on the arm of the chair, turned it over, palm up, as if he thought there might be something in it; then, with a wondering expression, he looked up at me. It seemed the whole room had begun to pound with noise, but then I understood it was my heart pounding in my ears. All I could think was, do not move and this moment will pass.

So it did. In the next Master said, "You may go now, Mary. I won't detain you from your work any longer."

I bobbed a curtsy, still unable to speak, and went out the door as fast as I could without seeming to bolt. In the hall I had to stop and lean against the wall, for my heart was racing so I could not get my breath, though now that I write it all down and think what really happened, I can't say just why I should have been so afraid.

This morning I was up early and in good spirits, for the first thing I saw was a beam of yellow sunlight coming into our attic through the window and falling across the bed onto the floor as if it was spilled from a pitcher. When I looked out the window I saw the sky was still pink but it would soon be all blue for there was not a cloud to be seen, nor were the treetops rustling, so the wind had gone and left us with a fine October day. Cook was up when I got to the kitchen, seeming cheerful as well, and even Mr. Poole, when he come in, did not have his gloomy air about him, though I doubt it is in his nature ever to be lighthearted. He said Master was up and would have his breakfast in the drawing room, for he was already working at his desk. I gulped down my tea standing near the stove, then put on my apron to go see to Master's fire. Walking along the hall was a fine sight, for the sun was streaming through the stained-glass windows making beams of red and green and gold, so clear I could pick them out. I knocked at the drawing room and Master bid me come in. As I worked at the grate Master said, "Well, Mary, your weather prediction was accurate. It is certainly a fine day."

"Yes, sir," I said. "It do lift the spirits."

"It does indeed," Master said, folding up a sheet of paper he'd been writing on and taking up another. Then, as he said no more to me, I finished my work and went back to the kitchen. All the way I could not help thinking, there is more to be grateful for than fine weather this morning, for we have all of us seen the last of Mr. Edward Hyde. And indeed when we sat down to breakfast in the kitchen, though we did not speak of it, I seemed to hear relief in our voices, even Mr. Poole's. It was the absence of Edward Hyde we could feel, as if he'd been taking up the air so we could not breathe it and now we drank it in in great gulps, which seems odd, as we had none of us much to do with him when he was here. The only sharp note sounded among us came when I told Mr. Poole Master had given me leave to see to my mother's funeral on Thursday. He remarked that it was not my place to ask for leave as it put Master on the spot, but I said, "I did not ask him, sir. He brought it up and all I said was it would be on Thursday and he said, then you must go." Mr. Poole pursed his lips at me in a way I don't like, but he said no more on the subject so I felt I'd got off easy.

The rest of the day I filled with work, and I could have filled another with ease. I did four tubs of laundry in the yard, all the table linens and bed sheets, as well as napkins and dish towels. I cleaned the silver Mr. Poole had put out, for he says Master is having seven to dinner Friday eve, so it is not too soon to start. I shook out the doormat, washed the front steps and did the brass. Then, as Master had gone out for the day, after lunch I dusted the drawing room and the library, swept out the carpets with tea leaves, also swept out the hall.

It did me good to work hard all day. At dinner I felt weary but in a pleasing way, so I thought, I will sleep well tonight. When Mr. Bradshaw come in he said he'd been out to the bootmaker and the newsmen was crying for Mr. Edward Hyde on every corner. "He will have left the country, if he's any sense at all," Mr. Bradshaw said. "Unless I miss my guess."

I said nothing but Mr. Poole put in, "I hear the

police have got to the bank before him, so he will not be able to draw the funds to make good his escape."

Cook sighed. "Oh, I hope he is gone," she said. "Or that he is soon apprehended. I only saw him that once, coming along near the court, but I have never got over the bad feeling it gave me. I believe I knew he was a cold-blooded murderer the moment I saw him."

"It is a pity," Mr. Poole said, "that our master's generous heart was taken in by such a creature as this Mr. Edward Hyde. But thank the Lord, I believe he now sees the danger he was in."

So I sat and said nothing, but I thought, no doubt he come to this house to get enough money from Master to make his escape. And then I thought, however much it was, in my view it was money well spent.

BOOK 3

This is a new book I bought at Lett's for sevenpence.

Today I was up early and worked until ten, for there was a deal to do in the house to have it ready for Master's dinner party tomorrow. I got all the folding done and ready for ironing, which I will do in the morning. It was a fine clear day like yesterday, a great relief to me as I had to cross the town, and also as I thought a funeral in the rain or fog would be so gloomy I could not bear up under it. I put on my dark skirt and grey bonnet and my mourning bands, also my heavy cloak, for there is a chill in the air though it is bright. Cook gave me a slice of mutton pie she had left from yesterday's lunch and a piece of brown bread which I wrapped up to take along.

So I went off and made my way through the busy streets. The bright day seemed to put the whole population in a good humour, and even the horses weaving through the traffic with their carts and cabs had a festive look about them. As I was standing at a crossing before Russell Square, a big grey fellow who was drawn up next me stretched out his long neck and took up a bit of my cloak in his lips, as if he wanted to have a look at it. When I started, he did too, throwing up his head, and the driver shouted down to me, "He's taken a fancy to you, miss," so I laughed and the big horse hung his head down as if he was ashamed.

I stopped near noon and ate my lunch at Finsbury Square, then drank a cup of milk from the man there and went on to Marm's lodgings.

Mr. Haffinger had done himself up in an outlandish costume which he seemed to think was very fine. He'd an old top hat, very high, such as one rarely sees these days, and a shabby cutaway coat that had seen better days. His waistcoat was too tight for him and his shirt had a high stiff collar, which he'd wrapped round three or four times with a black cravat so wide it came to the tip of the collar, so he looked as if he could neither breathe nor turn his head. He was pleased to see me, he said, and we was to go at once to the funerary furnishers, for they'd come to take Marm early in the morning and said they would be ready to proceed to the churchyard at one sharp. As we walked along he told me something that fair made me fall down in the street. He said that after I'd come to see him a gentleman visited him as well, asking after my marm. He would not give his name but said he was her relation and Mr. Haffinger took him down to his hole in the wall to look at her. The gentleman seemed very moved, Mr. Haffinger said, and asked after the funeral arrangements, which he was pleased to tell him was all settled by the daughter of the deceased. "Ah, Mary," the gentleman said, "so she has taken care of it." Mr. Haffinger told him the time of the funeral and suggested that he attend but the gentleman declined saying, "I do not think Mary would want to see me there." Then he gave Mr. Haffinger a sovereign to spend on feathers and went away.

"How can this be?" I said. "My marm had no relations that I know of, certain none as would know me by name."

"I cannot say," he replied. "Only I'm telling you what the gentleman said."

"But what was he like?" I said.

Here Mr. Haffinger brought out a long description: he was elderly, though perhaps not, but only worn down from hard work and illness, for he had a cough that never let up so he could scarcely carry on a conversation; his hair was dark, though perhaps it was grey, he had not marked it. He believed he was clean-shaven though there may have been some whiskers. His clothes was neat but not fashionable, a workingman's clothes, he thought, or perhaps a tradesman. He was not tall nor short, and so on until I thought I would scream at him. My head was pounding with the thought it must have been my father, though it were an outrage he should turn up at this unhappy time in the guise of a concerned relation; in fact, I could not bear to think on it. The description Mr. Haffinger gave me could have been anyone, so it could have been him, and I remembered with a shudder that he had always a cough.

No, I thought, half of London has a cough. This must surely be some cousin or uncle of Marm's that I know nothing of. But why then would he think I would not care to see him? Mr. Haffinger dug in his coat pocket and came out with the sovereign. "Here it is," he said. "You see, just as he gave it me." We had reached the funeral establishment and Mr. Haffinger stood holding out the sovereign to me at the doorway.

"Sir," I said. "You are an honest man. As I do not know this gentleman, I cannot accept his money. I beg you to keep it with my thanks."

This pleased the poor old fool no end and he repeated that he was indeed an honest man several times as we went in the door, and he was on the point of telling the undertaker the whole story but this gentleman, all wrapped in black and full of his own importance, cut him off to say the coach was pulled up and we was to proceed to the yard. But first we settled up the bill, which money I had brought with me, and I was given a copy with the price of everything down to the nails listed on it. Then we went out and it was a comfort to me to see that, though there was nothing fancy about it, the coach was a respectable one, the coffin a sound-looking box that did not look as if it would split open before it was in the ground, the bearers was not staggering from drink nor making a show with their pocket handkerchiefs of a grief they could not feel, and the horses was not run down but a quiet pair, well matched and not inclined to bolt through the streets as I have seen happen. We set out to the church—not a long walk, but I had time to think over this strange business of the man who came to look upon my marm, though I could make no sense on it. Mr. Haffinger walked alongside me, keeping his eye on the children who ran along beside us trying to see the coffin, as well as all the passersby who stopped at the sight of our procession to doff a hat or cease idle chatter, for the sight of the hearse do seem to sober the most frivolous folk. At the church the old vicar was waiting, and after he said a few prayers we was off to the churchyard, a dismal place where the graves is mostly not marked and five or six deep, but there is a poor chestnut tree in one corner and a newer section opened up this last year, Mr. Haffinger told me, with the new laws what allows for more space between, and here was where they brought Marm's coffin. As the vicar was saying a few words, for he knew Marm

enough to speak well of her, I looked over the grave-
yard, thinking perhaps this mysterious gentleman might
show his face, but I saw no one. I felt such comfort in
the poor ceremony I had got up to mark Marm's passing
that I saw why people do make so much of a funeral,
and I was grateful it was a clear, bright day and felt that
Marm might at last have some peace, for she had none
to speak of in her life.

Before we come away I gave the vicar a black silk
handkerchief and the undertaker gave me a remem-
brance card which was engraved with a willow at one
corner, I thought a pretty picture though there was no
such tree anywhere near that I could see.

Mr. Haffinger walked out to the street with me,
seeming awed by the spectacle, for he did not say a
word but wrung his hands, so I had no doubt he'd something on his mind and I should soon hear it. At the gate
I thanked him for being a friend to my marm and said I
must be off as I wanted to be back at my employment
by dinner.

"Before you go, miss," he said, "there's something
I must tell you. As you say, I am an honest man and it
will be on my conscience if I do not."

I told him he must speak freely then.

"So I must," he said, "or I shall have no rest. The
gentleman what come to see your poor ma was your
father."

My heart seemed to sink in my chest at these
words. "I thought as much," was all I said.

"He said there was bad feeling between you and that he was sorry for it. He is very bad off hisself and from the look of him will not live the winter, so he said hisself."

"You did not tell him where I lodge?" I said.

"That I did not, miss," he said. "He did not ask."

"Then I beg you, Mr. Haffinger, let that be an end to it."

"It do seem a shame, miss," he said, "that some old quarrel should not be patched over when so much time has passed and he is now a poor, lonely old fellow at death's door. Your poor ma had made her peace with him, why cannot you?"

"What makes you think my marm had made peace with him?" I said.

"Because he come to see her, more than once, in her illness and she did not send him away."

This made my blood pound in my ears. Words leaped to my lips and I snapped them out at Mr. Haffinger. "If she did not send him away," I said, "it were because she was afraid of him."

Mr. Haffinger seemed surprised at my response. "Afraid of *him?*" he repeated, as if it was not to be thought on. "That poor harmless old gentleman? And sick himself too, near to death. No, miss, I do not think you ma was afeared of your father. It were a case of two near dying at the same moment."

So, I thought, she never got free of him and even as she left this life he was there. With his last strength he hunted her down and she was too weak herself to do aught but his will, as it was always between them, only now his will was that he should be forgiven.

"Mr. Haffinger," I said, "do you feel certain my father will not live?"

He brightened at this as he thought my heart must be softening. "That he cannot, miss. He is coughing blood and he said he was in hospital, but was turned out for they said there was naught they could do for 'im."

I looked back at the yard where the gravediggers had come out, looking as black as the earth they deal in, and was struggling to get Marm's coffin in the hole they'd dug for her. Was it possible, I thought, my father believed what lay between us was only bad feeling? Did he truly imagine because he was dying I would want to see his face, to patch things over, as Mr. Haffinger put it? I looked at my hands which ached with these thoughts and then looked at Mr. Haffinger's wrinkled, wide-eyed face in his ridiculous funeral getup, near teary-eyed with the fancy he was to give a poor dying man back his lost daughter, and I set my jaw tight to keep a shout of laughter coming out. I wished I might have Master with me, who would understand better than anyone my feelings and would doubtless know what best to say. When I overcome my wish to laugh and the anger what followed on that, I said, as calm as I could, "Promise me, sir, you will not tell him where I lodge."

His hopeful face clouded with worry, but he give

me his word and so solemn like I knew he would keep it.

"Then let it rest, Mr. Haffinger," I said, and I took his hand in mine and shook it to seal the promise, and so left him standing in the bright sunshine to puzzle on just what could turn a heart so cold as mine.

*I*t has been many days since last I wrote. We have all of us been so run off our feet with work there has been no time, nor have I thought much of what I might want to tell, for at the end of the day I have gone up to bed weary to the bone and off to sleep as soon as I close my eyes.

Two times have I dreamed of my father and in both dreams he was not the cruel tyrant of my memory, but an old man, stooped and weak, a threat to no one, and in both he has tried to speak to me, but I have turned away. So I woke feeling a fine resolve, and I think perhaps right now he is dying somewhere, beaten and friendless, while I am safe in my bed.

I do not think my heart is hard but only that my reason has not gone soft, as seems to happen to so many at the thought of old age and illness, then death, which is what we mun each look forward to, whether we have lived well or badly. Sometimes when I am on the street and I see poor old men crouched in doorways in their rags and filth, begging for a penny, I want to look deep into their bleary eyes and ask, was there a child cried for mercy and you showed her none? Then here is a penny for her memory.

For I know what a lie old age makes of a life—indeed, it is the most fearsome part—and that my father would doubtless deny—nay, would not even remember—how cruel he used me. Now he does not want to die alone, so he makes up a daughter who could care for him and calls the rift between us "bad feeling."

My fear of him is gone and in its place anger, which fills my head so at times I can scarce find my away about. So I keep at my writing, for two reasons: one that it eases me to write what I do not say, for no one cares enough to hear it—that I do remember and, though I do not hate him I do not forgive him; and second that if I write it now, then it cannot be denied in future. Will I ever be myself so muddled that I will soften the long horror that was my childhood and tell myself perhaps it was not so bad? Let this book serve as my memory.

*A*nother week has passed. Master has had a stream of visitors, coming at all hours, sometimes expected and sometimes not, so Cook says she has put out more food in five days than in the whole month previous.

The weather turns cooler every day, it seems to me, though we have had two days' sun for a few hours in the afternoon when Cook and I took time to work in our garden, putting in all manner of bulbs which Mr. Bradshaw got from his aunt who lives in the country. I never knew before how these go in the ground before it freezes and stay there all the winter long—storing up food, Cook says, until they know somehow it is safe to come up, though some, as crocuses and snowdrops, come very early and often show their bright colours through a frost. Many of our flowers will not winter, Cook says, and so mun come out, though the herbs is mostly more hardy and may stay. We turned the back section under, adding lime, a full afternoon's work, which I was glad to have. Indeed I cannot get enough of working and make up projects if there is nothing to hand, so Cook says I am like a squirrel hurrying about, storing up things and getting everything in order, for winter is fast upon us.

I do feel pressed, but it is not winter that is closing in upon me. True, the days is shorter and there is less light and it is cold, so it comes as no surprise that I spend my time cleaning lamps and hauling up coal— still, I feel always it is not enough. I had a fancy last night as I was trimming the drawing-room lamps that I would take every lamp in the house and light them in one room and then, if I stood among them, I might see properly.

This evening Master is out to a meeting and then a dinner having to do with his project for a Latin school for workingmen, which he has got underway with Mr. Littleton, who, he says, has to be bullied every step of the way. Master has not set foot in his laboratory for weeks, but is occupied completely in his good works, so when he is not having gentlemen in or going out to them, he is writing letters. His good spirits and energy keep us all in a like mood, so even Mr. Poole, who likes nothing better than to greet gentlemen at the door and then tell us their family tree or all their connections in the government, is in a tolerable frame of mind. We have heard nothing of Mr. Edward Hyde—Master does not speak of him, nor has the police caught up with him, so he must have escaped the country, as Mr. Bradshaw said he might, which I pray is what happened so that we will see him no more.

*M*any days has passed. Last night Master had a small dinner party, Mr. Utterson, Mr. Littleton and Dr. Lanyon, who went to school with Master, so Mr. Poole says, but has not visited here in some years. Master sent word to Cook to put on something "really fine," even though the party was small, which seemed to please her as she says it is sometimes a pleasure to do things with style, so she did six courses—a soup with chopped spinach, soles in brown gravy, pigeons stewed, saddle of mutton, potatoes, salad, and soufflé. The kitchen was in as much of a ruction as if we'd had ten to dine and poor Annie groaned every time Cook took down another pot, for she has spent more time scrubbing these last weeks than sleeping, which don't suit her, and I've no doubt she wishes Master would go back to his solitary ways and his late night plate of cold mutton. The rest of us was enjoying the activity, especially Mr. Poole, who had a long confab with Master over the wine and brought the bottles out one at a time, dusting them off and going over the labels with Mr. Bradshaw as if he was showing off the crown jewels. There was seven bottles, also champagne and port, which I thought should set the gentlemen up to a very late hour, so I got in a good lot of coal to the dining room, drawing room and front hall, as it is a chilly night out, though clear, and wine do thin the blood. I had the fires going before they arrived, so the rooms was comfortable and they spent more than an hour in the drawing room before they went in to dine. I had on my best black woollen skirt and gabardine blouse, what I got for my mourning, a clean apron and a new cap, my mourning bands, and I felt very smart, for the new skirt is narrower in the fashion, so it is easier to move about without a fuss. I was to go up with Mr. Poole to hand round the soup, which made me anxious, as I do not like to wait at table, for all the gentlemen see of me is my hands and they are rough-looking no matter how I might scrub them. Cook seemed to know my feelings, for as I stood smoothing my apron she said, "You look fine, Mary. The new cap suits you." So I took up the tray and followed Mr. Poole and Mr. Bradshaw, who had the tureen, up the stairs, feeling I was going onto a stage and did not know my part.

But when we went in I was soon at my ease, for the gentlemen was talking to one another all at once, it seemed, and paid us no mind. Their conversation was on the subject of Master's project for a Latin school, and the three gentlemen, Mr. Utterson, Mr. Littleton and Master, was at persuading Dr. Lanyon to join them in it. Dr. Lanyon seemed to me a gloomy gentleman and I did not like the way he spoke to Master, for it seemed every time Master spoke he contradicted him, while when the others spoke, he agreed. He said it was enough that he gave part of his time to the free hospital, where Mr. Utterson and Mr. Littleton could be of no use, for they was not medical men. "But you, Harry," he said, "might remember your oath and do as much good with me as in your Latin school." So Master said, "I will gladly give you hour for hour in your hospital, if you will join us in this school."

I would have thought this would be an end of it, but then it seemed Dr. Lanyon had some objection to the school beyond his feeling he was not suited to it, for he only said he would think upon it. They all fell upon their soup and the subject changed, but before I could make it out, we was done serving and went down.

Then I was busy in the kitchen, helping Cook, laying out the platters and silver, stirring the pots as she directed and handing all manner of things to Mr. Poole and Mr. Bradshaw, who was up and down the stairs a dozen times. I saw two more bottles of wine go up and then the champagne with the soufflé, after which we all breathed a sigh and Cook flung herself down in the chair and said, "My poor knees must have a rest." It was not long after this that Mr. Bradshaw called me up to help with the clearing off. The gentlemen was rising from the meal as I come in and indeed Mr. Utterson and Dr. Lanyon were nearly out the door, for Mr. Utterson knows his way to the drawing room and has said many times how he likes to sit before Master's fire after a good meal. Master was speaking to Mr. Littleton and I heard him say, "Hastie has always taken a dim view of my enthusiasms. He thinks it is his duty," very wry-seeming and loud enough for Dr. Lanyon to hear, though I think he did not, for I looked at his back going out and he gave no sign of it. Then when I looked back Mr. Littleton was walking out but Master had stopped and to my surprise I found he was looking at me with a very amused expression, for he'd read in my eyes what I think of Dr. Lanyon. So I ducked my head to my work, which was taking up plates. Master said to Mr. Poole, "Tell Cook she has outdone herself, Poole," and then he went out.

After that we was all busy for more than an hour clearing up, and I helped Annie scour the pots for which she was grateful. She was yawning like a cat and no sooner was the last done then she went up to bed saying she hoped we would have no more gentlemen in ever, which made Cook scowl at her and say she was spoiled from Master's quiet ways and should not last a fortnight in a country house, which was nothing but dinners and parties. "Nor would I," was all Annie said and went on climbing the stairs, yawning at every step so we had to laugh at her. Mr. Poole come down then and took a seat saying everything was done for a spell, but I was to go and tend the fire, as it was very low, so I went up. I found the drawing-room door open. I looked in to see Mr. Utterson, Mr. Littleton and Dr. Lanyon had drawn their chairs into half a circle facing the fire and Master stood next to it, leaning his arm on the mantel, so he saw me at the door and said, "Come in, Mary. As you can see, we need you, for I am trying to climb into the chimney."

So all the gentlemen looked up at me as I went in, which made me uncomfortable. I went to the grate, knelt down before it and went straight to work, which seemed to make me invisible, for they went back to their conversation at once. It was Dr. Lanyon who was speaking, to this end, that it was not a good thing to educate the working classes for it gave them ideas above their station and could only lead to more discontent in lives already difficult to bear. "To a man who spends his every waking moment in some sweatshop where there is neither light nor air, and thereby earns scarcely enough to feed his family, it is a greater service that he may bring his ruined eyes and weakened lungs to hospital then to some ill-lit room where you would teach him to read a language he can never use and to entertain notions that

can only make him more keenly aware of the hopelessness of his station." Indeed, he went on, it was a wonder
to him that Master could find *any* students foolhardy
enough to attend such a school, and that he could only
proved the incurable foolishness and obstinacy of the
class.

Master said surely the spirit could starve as well as
the body, and Mr. Littleton put in that there was a great
demand for the school and that he found the men to be
eager for knowledge. Mr. Utterson said his students
copied his manners as well as his lessons and he could
not see that it could harm a workingman to know how
to comport himself among gentlemen.

While all this was being said, I had finished my
work and the fire was blazing up so high it seemed my
face would catch, but I could not move without inter-
rupting the stream of talk, which seemed, as Mr. Utterson concluded, to pause for a moment while Dr. Lanyon
drew his breath to reply.

"To what end, Gabriel?" he said, in such an angry
voice we all seemed to draw away from his harsh tone.
"To what end this sham of gentility? So that a rogue
may call a gentleman by his Christian name before he
throttles him to death with another gentleman's walking
stick?"

Then we could have heard a pin drop on the carpet,
the silence was that sudden and thick. I kept my eyes
on the grate but I heard Master lift his glass from the
mantel, drink from it, then set it back down very slow,
and when he spoke his voice was the same, slow and

careful. "We differ only on interpretation, Hastie," Master said. "We always have. You see the exception and conclude it proves the rule. What I fear is that unless we make some effort to bring the light of reason to the labouring classes, that exception may well *be* the rule."

Dr. Lanyon, who seemed ashamed of what he had said, as well he might be, mumbled a few words to the effect that Master might have a point.

"Can we agree on this, then," Master said, "that as we gather here, comfortable, safe and warm after a good meal, with our fire and our port and you, Gabriel, with your pipe, a new world is coming into being just outside there." Here Master lifted his glass to the window that faces the square. "And it is a world we know little about, one that may have no place for us in it, a world"—Master paused and all the gentlemen hung on his words, as did I—"we made ourselves but which is already beyond our control."

Dr. Lanyon spoke up at once. "Aye," he said. "That is the truth."

They fell quiet again until Master said to Mr. Utterson, "Gabriel, your glass is empty. May I fill you another?" Then I took the opportunity to get up off my knees and slip out, feeling I'd overheard more than I could understand. As I went downstairs I went over what each gentleman had said and pondered what Master might mean by saying that the world might have no place for him in it. I was struck with how mild he had responded to Dr. Lanyon's remark, for surely he had meant Master was in some way to blame for the murder of Sir Danvers Carew, because he had tried to do good among those who could not profit by it. In the kitchen I took off my apron and Mr. Poole told me he would close up and I might go off to bed, which I did, taking a fresh candle with me so that I would have light to set down these things I heard.

It do seem as the days grow shorter there is less time and more to fill it with, so the hours go by and I am too weary of an evening to write in my journal and of a morning too busy. Master is in and out at all hours, but has not gone to his laboratory in many weeks, for he has so many of what Mr. Poole calls his "projects" afoot it is all he can do to keep up with them. The weather is cold, full of gloom, though the holiday season will be upon us soon and the shops bring out all manner of things to sell, earlier each year, so it is bright and pleasant to walk among them. Our garden is bloomed out and laid down for spring, so Cook says we will have little work in it for the next two months. We have dried a good many herbs and potted up some smaller ones to bring in.

Days go by and Master hardly speaks to me, so I find myself waiting eagerly to be summoned to stir up a fire or carry some message downstairs and always come away feeling sad, for he only says what must be said and does not ask after me or seem to want my opinion, but has his mind always occupied with matters outside our house. Indeed he is in good spirits most of the time and he is by his nature such a thoughtful gentleman no one in his service could ever count himself ill used. Yet I feel somehow he does not like to see me, for I remind him of that house in Soho, which I wish I had never seen, and of his unhappy connection with one who betrayed his confidence and trust so cruel and open for all the world to see. Many times as I am going out of a room I look back to see him working at his desk or pacing about before the fire and I want to say, He is gone. Must he still stand between us?

But I know there is no help for it. Mr. Edward Hyde will never leave us. Everything we do in this house is to cover the place where he is still. The way we never speak of him speaks of him. I never enter a room but I expect to find him there. Even now, sitting quietly at the end of day with my candle and my journal, I seem to hear his strange light footstep on the stair.

*S*omething is amiss, though I do not know what. Yesterday Master went out in the afternoon on some errand, saying he would not be back until dinner. Then, very close to dinnertime, a note was handed in to

Mr. Poole from Master, saying he would not be back until very late but that Dr. Lanyon would be coming by to take something from his cabinet. Mr. Poole was to engage a locksmith to open the door. Even Mr. Poole, who never questions Master's wishes, said to Cook, "It is odd he did not send the key," but Cook said, "He has not been in his laboratory in so long, mayhap he has mislaid it." So Mr. Poole did as Master asked and Dr. Lanyon came by after dinner, but I did not see him. Then we all finished our chores and sat about waiting for Master. I helped Annie cut out a dress pattern. At eleven Master still had not come, so Mr. Poole said we had all best turn in and he would get up if Master rung for anything. None of us heard him come in, but in the morning when Mr. Poole come down he said Master was asleep and we was not to disturb him. We crept about all the morning, until Mr. Poole came out and found me doing the brass on the street, to say Master wanted a fire in his room, for he was not feeling well enough to come down.

So I went up and tapped at the door, and Master called out, "Come in." He was huddled in his chair before the cold grate with the lap robe over his legs and another thrown around his shoulders. He gave me a weary smile as I come in and I thought he looked old of a sudden, as if his night out had taken years off his life. "Mary," he said, "I think I'm frozen through."

"Oh, I'm sorry, sir," I said. "I was not certain whether to leave a fire last night but Mr. Poole said he would get up when you come in, so I did not."

"I did not wake him," Master said. "I was so tired, I was asleep as soon as I got to my bed and I've only just waked up."

I knelt down before the coals and went to work. "Cook is sending you up a tray," I said. "A cup of tea will bring you right."

Master sighed. "I wish that were true," was all he said.

It did not take long to get the coals going, then I went to draw the curtains for the sun was shining, though it was cold, and I thought the light might make Master feel less dreary. I noticed a drawer sitting on the floor near the window, which had some odd-looking bottles as for medicine, as well as papers such as is drawn up at the chemist's, though not marked. It looked like the drawers in the press in Master's cabinet and I thought it must be, so this was doubtless what Dr. Lanyon had come for and Master had met with him to bring it back. I stepped around it to reach the curtains but Master said, "No, Mary. Leave them closed." Then Mr. Poole come in with the tray and began fussing over Master, so I went out. When Mr. Poole come down he told Mr. Bradshaw he was going out to fetch the locksmith again and Master was not at home to any visitors for the rest of the day.

When the locksmith come in the afternoon, Master went out to his laboratory with him and they was busy there some time, replacing the lock what was taken off yesterday with a new one, so Cook told me. After our tea Mr. Poole come from upstairs to say Master wished to speak to me in the drawing room, so I went up at once. Master was just finishing his own tea when I come in and he looked better than he had in the morning, but he seemed anxious and even vexed, for he come straight to the point as soon as I come in. "I want you to give my cabinet a thorough cleaning, Mary," he said. I know my mouth dropped open for I never thought to hear such a request from Master. He paid me no mind but fished out the key from his pocket and held it out to me. "I've told Poole this is your first priority."

"Yes, sir," I said.

"I'll be spending a good deal of time there these next weeks and it's very dusty from disuse. I'm sure you'll find your work cut out for you."

"Yes, sir," was all I said.

"Put in some coal in the theatre, so I can get to it with ease."

"I will, sir," I said. Then as I was going out he said, "Don't bother to clean the theatre, Mary. Just the cabinet."

I looked back at him and glad I was that I did, for he gave me a most kind smile and said, "If I turn you loose upon the place you'll have everything sparkling in no time. Don't touch those cobwebs in the theatre. I don't want to be attacked by disgruntled spiders."

I laughed at this and went on my way, feeling my spirits much lifted by Master's easy way as well as the opportunity to do some real service to him. I was soon among my buckets and brushes, choosing the best for each purpose, and I mixed up a special polish, for I thought I might make those smiling babies on the fender glow like lamps with a bit of effort. Cook laughed at me and said to Mr. Poole, who passed through the kitchen looking testy, for he hates anything like a change, "Mary thinks it a holiday to finally have a go at Master's cabinet." Then I went into the yard and began drawing water. It was cold out but fair and as I passed the garden to bring the buckets to the theatre door, I thought about the bulbs storing up food under the soil and waiting for the time when they knew it would be safe to push up. How odd it is that plants can have what we so often do without—good sense and judgement. I set down my buckets and took out the key Master give me, for I thought I should have a look at the room before I brought the rest of my things along, to decide how to proceed. The theatre door had been left open, so I walked in.

The afternoon light was thin and feeble, so it seemed to give out before it reached the floor, leaving much of the big room in darkness. The boxes and packing straw that stood about gave off a strong smell of damp and decay. I crossed to the stairs, thinking I should have to bring a lamp in as well, and slipped the key into the shiny new lock. When I opened it I found the cabinet darker still, for the curtains was drawn, so I went to open them at once. There was a thick, dry smell of dust, not of damp as in the theatre, and when I touched the curtains I knew at once that they would have to come down, for as I moved them aside the air was filled with dust. The windows here was not so blackened as those in the theatre, though they was by no means clean, and the light came streaming in, so I thought, best start with this so I can see to do the rest. When I looked back at the room it seemed a wonder that a few months of being closed up had caused so much dust, for I always think it is shoes that bring it in, but there was balls of dust in the corners and under the furniture. If I get the curtains and carpets out this evening, I thought, and work all day tomorrow, I could have it done by evening. I saw that the press had a drawer missing, so my guess was right. Master had for some reason sent for it, then brought it back with him. I heard footsteps in the court and looked out to see two gentlemen walking by and talking to each other very earnestly, though I could not hear what they said. I found a straight chair in the corner, which I drew up to the windows. When I climbed upon it I could just reach the tops of the curtains, so I began taking them down while the dust rose in a cloud about me and went straight up my nose. It made me dizzy, also my eyes began to water and all at once I had the feeling someone was watching me. When I turned round I saw it was my own reflection in the cheval glass, looking back at me with a frightened expression, so I felt I had been foolish and went back to my work feeling chided.

I got the curtains down, the carpets hung up in the yard and the windows washed before it was dark. Then I brought in a lamp, cleared a space near the stairs and begun to put in the coal, as I thought there was no point in cleaning by lamplight. As I was carrying the last scuttle across the yard I heard the kitchen door open and Master came out. He had put his coat on and walked up to me at once. The scuttle was heavy, I was weary and black from my work, so I only said, "Good evening, sir," and kept my eyes down while he fell into step beside me. When we had got inside, I put down the scuttle and rubbed my hands on my apron. Master was looking about the theatre, which seemed huge and full of shadows darting about in the lamplight. "So," Master said, seeming to talk to himself, for he did not look at me, "the final act will be played out in this poor theatre." Then he sighed and turned his attention to me.

"I beg your pardon, sir?" I said.

But Master ignored my question. "How does your work progress?" he asked.

"Well enough, sir," I said. "I will be done by tomorrow eve."

Then Master said nothing but stood looking down at me, so I felt embarrassed, for I knew my face was smeared with black and my hair was straying from my cap. I put my hand up to push it back but still Master did not stop looking at me and I thought he had something in mind to say but did not say it. At last I could not bear the silence longer so I spoke. "I'm not fit to be seen, sir," I said.

Then Master put out his hand and touched my

cheek. His fingers went at once to the scar near my ear and then to the other on my throat. "I was thinking how dear your face is to me, Mary," he said. "And how sad it would make me if I were never to see it more."

I could scarce believe my ears to hear Master speak so, nor could I reply for a moment, only I shook my head to say no, that could not be. While his hand moved back to my cheek, he looked up at the cabinet door and his eyes seemed to fill with a sadness deeper still. Then he drew his hand away. "I'm afraid, Mary," he said. "I'm afraid of what comes next."

"How can I help you, sir?" I said.

For a moment he looked as if he was thinking over some plan, but then his eyes seemed to go hard and he said, "No one can help me." He turned away and walked to the door, while I stood in such a state of confusion and fear, trying to understand what he might mean, I thought my head would burst, only I saw he was leaving and I could not bear it. Without knowing I was about to speak I called to him, but I used the name I always give him in my thoughts, though I have never spoke it to him before. "Master," I cried out.

He stopped and turned to me while the word hung in the air between us, and he smiled a little as he thought upon it. "Yes, Mary," he said.

"I will not leave you," I said.

"Good," he replied. Then he went out into the cold, dark yard and without looking back at me, crossed it and let himself into the house at the kitchen door.

oday is grey, wet, so cold it seems to go through to the bones. After breakfast the first thing I did was to get a fire in Master's cabinet, for I thought if I did not my hands would freeze up on me and I would not be able to work. These last weeks, as it grows colder, I've had a numbness in my fingers what worries me. I did the windows first, so what miserable daylight there is could come into the room. Then I set to work on the floors. I worked all morning and by noon I had made a difference and the room begun to look as if someone cared for it. At lunch Mr. Poole said Master was not feeling at all well and planned to spend the day in his room or in the library, for he wanted some books packed up and brought out to the cabinet. Again he told Mr. Bradshaw Master was not at home to any callers.

We all looked at one another having the same thought. Master is going back to his work. Cook would have no dinner parties to get up, Annie no big pots to scrub, Mr. Poole no gentlemen to talk about, Mr. Bradshaw no evening clothes to lay out and I would not have to wait at table or run out on errands because all hands was filled. Instead we will go back to our old way and our work will be to keep Master in good health, for he does not care for himself.

In the afternoon I got the curtains, which I brushed last night, back up and the carpets down. I could not stop thinking of what Master said to me yesterday and my feelings was a jumble, for I know not what Master means, or what he is afraid of, and seeing him so disturbed makes me sad, yet his kind words to me, especially his saying that I am dear to him and the memory of his cool hand against my face, these make my heart race and I feel, I cannot deny it, so happy for it, it is almost like a pain.

I saved the brass for last and though it was all clean enough it had been a long time since any polish had been put on. It gave me a great pleasure to polish the laughing babies on the fender and when I was done it was such a difference to stand before the grate it made me laugh, for their faces is that gay they seem like two children romping in the sun, all golden from it.

By evening I was done and I began hauling all my cleaning things down to the theatre. Then I went back up to the cabinet to look at my work.

It was still like two rooms, one the comfortable sitting room of a gentleman, the other, where the long table stood on the bare floor, the workplace of a man of science. There was not too many bottles and strange tubes upon the table, but what I found there I had washed up so they was sparkling, but the light they gave off was not pleasing. I wished I had a big vase of roses, such as we put in the dining room in the summer, to set in the middle of that table, which of course I could not get this time of year and no doubt I would not even have the nerve to do it, though Master would say nothing, only move them away.

As I was going out Mr. Bradshaw come into the

theatre carrying a box of books Master wanted from the library. He said Master was in a strange way in his view, wanting everything changed up and the cabinet fitted out as if he was moving house. "He has gone about this livelong day carrying that drawer of his," he said, "as if he thought someone would take it from him, and when Mr. Utterson come to the door he run up the stairs saying he was not at home, as if he thought we might say he was, when he'd given orders this morning that he was not."

"It must be he plans to take up some work as will not bear interruption," I said.

"You may say so," Mr. Bradshaw said, then we parted and he went to the cabinet and I to the yard.

After dinner I went up to the library to see to Master's fire. I found him sitting in his chair, gazing into a book and what Mr. Bradshaw said is true, he had the drawer from his cabinet on the floor next his chair. He asked if I was finished my work and I said, yes, it was done.

"Good, then," he said. "Tell Poole I will be working tonight. He needn't wait up for me."

That was all our conversation. When I had finished my work I went out. A little while later, as we all sat in the kitchen, though Mr. Poole was in his parlour, we heard Master go down the back stairs and out across the yard.

*L*ast night I woke up late and knew at once the sound I heard was Master's footsteps as he come in at the kitchen and went up the stairs. So, I thought, we are back to our old ways where I lie awake and listen while Master walks the night. He did not go up to his room but went along the hall to the library. Then for a time it was quiet and I thought I would drift back to sleep, but I could not stop straining for a sound. The house was so still I could hear Annie's breathing, though she hardly does breathe when she is asleep, nor does she move, so sometimes I touch her hand to make sure she is still warm. Then it seemed I heard another sound, like a low hum, seeming very far off, and I lifted my head from the pillow to try and take it in, but I could not place it. Still it went on, without any break. At last I sat up in the bed, for I seemed to know what it was but could not name it. "What is it?" I said, but softly, not to wake Annie.

I got up and opened our door so that I might make it out and indeed it did come in more clear but still I could not place it. I walked out to our landing and stood listening, then it come right up the stairs to me and I said, "It is voices."

But, I thought, that cannot be, for I heard only Master come in and there is no one else up, or else I would have heard them, though it is true that Mr. Poole can move along as soundless as a ghost; still, I thought,

I would have heard something, for this house has many creaks, especially on the stairs.

At last I could not bear it but thought I must know. Also it seemed that Master had been in the library some time, the fire was surely gone and the room cold, which was a reason to go down and look in. I could not go in my shift so I put my wool skirt on top and my grey blouse which was hung on the chair. I wrapped my hair up, sticking in a few pins to hold it back, then, taking up the candle, I went out into the hall. I did not bother with boots or stockings, for they take so long to put on, so I looked odd indeed, but I thought perhaps I would only go down to the hall and listen for a moment to set my mind at rest, so no one might see me after all.

When I got down the stairs I stopped again on the landing and listened. The light poured out into the hall, for the library door was open and now I understood what it was I heard. Master was reading out loud. I could not make out what he was saying but his voice was even and strong, forming the words and sentences with care. I went along and as soon as I crossed into the light Master saw me, for he was standing near the mantel and holding the book up before him, which I thought was surely an uncomfortable way to read.

"Mary," he said, "I did not hear you come along the hall."

"I'm sorry, sir, if I alarmed you," I said. "I heard voices and thought you might want a fire, as it is such a cold night." And without willing it I shuddered, for there was a draft at the door.

"It is indeed," Master said. "But I'll do without a fire. In fact I came in because my cabinet is so warm it made me drowsy."

This struck me as very odd, for I thought, it is not like Master to leave a warm room for a cold one and, as it was the middle of the night, if he felt drowsy why not go to his bed. I said nothing but stood staring at Master, feeling sleepy myself, and he held his book open, giving me a look I thought was like an apology, though I could not think what for. At last I said, "May I bring you something, sir? A pot of tea? Or something to eat?"

"No," Master said. "No, nothing, Mary." He rubbed one eye with the knuckles of his free hand. He looked weary to the bones, there was circles beneath his eyes and it seemed he was bent over a little, as if he could hardly hold himself up. "I'll only try to stay awake a little longer," he said. Then, as I watched him, a strange expression come to his face, as if he'd a sudden pain, so sharp he clenched his hands and in doing so, dropped the book. He did not try to pick it up but clutched the mantel. His face went white, his brow came out in a sweat and he let out a groan that went through me, so I bolted across the room to get to him, for it seemed in the next moment he would fall down. Indeed when I was near he clutched my arm and leaned his weight upon me, but did not speak, for I saw he could not. He put his other hand on my shoulder and his fingers dug in so hard it hurt, but I said nothing, for we was facing one another and his eyes was fastened on mine, full of pain and fear, but still with the look of apology, so I thought, he is ashamed for me to see him like this, but I held him up and held his gaze as steady as I could. Then it seemed a long time but mayhap it was only a moment, while the pain let up and he loosed his grip on me. He was too weak to stand, so I took a step and shifted his weight to my other shoulder, so that I could help him down into his chair. He fell forward, holding his head in his hands and taking in slow breaths, so I thought whatever it is has passed, but I did not move for fear he might faint dead away. He put his hands out before him and looked into his palms, still seeming dazed, and said, "I did it."

I said, "Sir?" for I did not understand him. I was standing so close in front of him he had to look up to see my face. "Ah, Mary," he said. "Thank you. I'm all right now." Then he looked back down and after a moment when I did not speak or move, he said, "Why, Mary. You've come down without your boots."

So I looked down and saw my bare toes sticking out beneath my skirt, which seemed a shocking sight, so I drew them back and said, "Oh, sir. I do beg your pardon."

But Master was smiling at me now, as if nothing could be more pleasing than my bare feet, and I felt so confused I came over red I'm sure. I took a few steps back, trying to keep my skirt over my feet, which was very awkward, and as I did we heard the clock strike three.

"Go to bed, child," Master said. "You've done all you can do for me tonight."

"Sir," I said, "are you sure you are well enough?"

"Yes," Master said. "Go along."

"Then good night, sir," I said and made a curtsy and as I went out Master said, "Good night, Mary."

I went along the hall feeling I could not sort out my thoughts. On the stairs I said, "He called me 'child,'" and I looked back down the steps thinking I did not like to leave him. When I was back in my bed I listened to hear him go up to his room, but I must have fallen asleep, for I did not hear another sound until I woke this morning.

There is no doubt Master is very ill and stays so much in his cabinet from being too weak to come into the house. He sends Mr. Poole out two or three times a day with orders to chemists so he is still at his work. Yesterday, when Cook was complaining that Master hardly ate the food she sent him and spent all his time doing his experiments, working his life away, Mr. Bradshaw said, "Perhaps he is working at something to make himself well." We was at dinner and all of us, even Mr. Poole, fell silent and looked at Mr. Bradshaw with surprise, for first none of us has ever gone so far as to say Master is ill, and second it seemed that this was a very good explanation for the strangeness we all feel. After a moment Mr. Poole said, "Mr. Bradshaw, I think you may be right."

So we finished our meal without saying more about it. Master never did come in from his laboratory last night. He took his breakfast near noon, which he had Mr. Poole bring out to him. When the tray came back this afternoon, Cook looked into all the dishes and muttered to herself, "A man cannot live on toast and tea," she said. "Look at this kipper. He has not touched it."

Poor Master. Cook put the kipper aside and sent it back again with his tea.

Three days has passed and Master has not come out of his laboratory. Even Mr. Poole has not seen him, though he goes back and forth, bringing his meals and carrying away his orders, which Mr. Poole finds on the stairs. He told Cook he always knocks when he brings the trays but Master only calls out, "Leave it, Poole. I can't come to the door now." Cook says his appetite is better, at least, for as often as not the dishes come back empty. All his visitors are turned away, even Mr. Utterson, who used to be let in without a question, but Mr. Poole has orders that no one must disturb Master so he only says Master is not to home.

We all feel something is amiss. It is like a fog rising up from the carpets, standing in every turning of the staircase. We carry on with our duties as best we can, for how can we do otherwise? but I think there is not an easy heart in this house.

Today I noticed that Mr. Poole leaves the key to the theatre on a nail in the pantry, for he goes in and out so often he mun have it close by. The key to the cabinet, which used to be on that ring, is not there.

I wish I was one who could find solace in prayer, but I am not. To put things down, that is my way, but I fear this time nothing will help me and I wonder is it safe even to *write* what I now know?

Last night I could not sleep. I lay awake waiting for the day to come but it seemed it never would. I went over all the events of these past weeks and especially of what Master said to me in the theatre, that I am dear to him and he should always want to see my face, and also of how sick he was in the library, and how he called me "child." Now he has been shut up in his cabinet for days and Mr. Poole says he only speaks when he has to and then sounds weak and peevish, so surely he is very ill. And I thought of how today was so unseasonable warm and clear, the sun seemed to pour into our windows like butter, so it seemed surely Master would want to sit outdoors, but then I wondered, does he even open the curtains in that room? It is as if he is in a tomb, shut away from all light and gaiety, what might do him more good than any medicine he can mix up on his laboratory table.

These thoughts went through my head for hours until I wanted to pull my hair out from going over them so often. At last I could stand it no longer and got up and lit a candle. I sat at the window for a few moments looking out at the rooftops and the stars, which was bright and it seemed so numerous I wondered had I ever seen so many. Then I only felt more restless and paced about in our room, trying not to wake Annie, until I decided I must get out and walk about, for I felt I was very large and the room was like a cage to me. I pulled on my wool stockings and put on my cloak over my shift. Then I went downstairs, carrying my boots, all the way to the kitchen, which was still warm from the oven, so I knew it could not be too late, though past midnight for I'd heard the clock strike when I lay awake.

I sat at the kitchen table and put on my boots, thinking all the time of the key Mr. Poole leaves in the pantry. I had it in my head to take it down, go into the theatre and knock at the cabinet door; in fact, I knew I had this thought in my head the first time I noted the key there, so it was this plan that now kept me up and I would not sleep until I carried it out. I slipped into the pantry as quiet as I could, took down the key and went out to the kitchen door. It has a latch that makes a noise when it is pulled—I hear it often enough when Master comes in—but I turned it very slow and careful so it did not make a sound and then I opened the door and stepped outside.

As soon as I did I heard something so odd I could not move before I had puzzled it out. Of course I looked to see where it was coming from but it was that dark I could make out nothing, so I had to trust my ears a moment longer. Then it come to me, it was weeping. Someone was weeping very low and going on and on, the way a child will sob, but it was too deep to be a child. My eyes began to find their way in the darkness and I made out a figure all wrapped in black, lying flat on the flags. He was on his back, looking up at the stars, though doubtless he could not see them for the tears, his arms stretched out at his sides as if he had been flung down there from a great height, and the strangled sobs that came from his throat poured out into the night, filling all the air with sadness. It must be Master, I thought, but somehow I knew it was not. He did not seem the right size, but much smaller and even as I had that thought I took a step forward. In doing so my boot made a sharp sound against the flag, he turned his face towards me and we knew each other.

I think I said, "Oh," and fell back against the door. He leapt to his feet in a whirl of motion, making a snarling sound like an animal, so I crouched down against the door for I thought he would run towards me, but instead he took a few steps backward towards the theatre door, then stopped. I put my hand over my mouth to keep from screaming and when he saw this his terror

2 3 3

disappeared. He dashed the tears from his eyes with his fists and shook his head as if to clear his thoughts. "Mary," he said. "Don't run. I won't harm you."

My heart seemed to be bursting through my chest and I had not the power of speech, so I stood another moment waiting for it to come to me. He did not move but watched me—wary, but I thought not angry. When I could speak I said, "What have you done to my master?"

He gave a snort of laughter and said, "Your master?" most contemptuous. "Better ask what he has done to me."

"Does he know you are here?" I said.

He looked over his shoulder at the theatre door, then back at me. "Come closer, Mary," he said. "I cannot hear you."

I could not think what to do. I could run back into the house and wake Mr. Bradshaw, but in the meantime he would be at liberty and might run away—or worse, do some harm to Master. He stood glaring at me, opening and closing his hands at his sides, and I thought, if I go closer what is to keep him from using them on my throat? But then I thought he would not, for he could not harm me without pointing a finger at himself, and once he was forced from Master's protection he knew as well as I, he would find no other hiding place but must run straight to the gallows. I cannot say all these thoughts came to my mind, only that I knew he would not dare to hurt me and so I came out from under the eave of the house and crossed the yard. I went towards him very slowly, holding my cloak tight about me. Though it was not a cold night, I felt chilled through and through and as I walked I clenched my jaw, for my teeth was chattering. He was on the far side of the garden and when I come to the edge of it, just out of his easy reach, I stopped. "Can you hear me now?" I said.

He drew himself up and gave me a horrid smile so his teeth seemed to flash like a knife in the darkness. "Quite the fearless little servant, aren't you Mary," he said. "Is there nothing you wouldn't face down for this master of yours?"

"Does he know you are here?" I said again.

He looked impatient, as if my question bored him, and before he spoke he sent his eyes running over me, which I felt like so many fingers of ice, and his upper lip lifted for a moment as if he'd as soon snarl as speak. "Of course," he said.

"You promised him you would go away," I said.

"I'm afraid that's easier said than done."

"You know he is ill," I said.

He laughed. "His life is in less danger than mine."

I looked toward the theatre and I saw the door stood partly open. I thought of making a run for it, but I feared he would catch me and I did not want him to touch me or think of me for one moment as his prey, for I knew if he did he would not be able to stop himself and if Master did not come out in time my life would be forfeit. He seemed to read my thoughts for he said, "You know, Mary, I'm a desperate man."

I looked back at him. It was then I noticed he was

wearing Master's clothes entire and that they was all too big for him, so he had rolled up the legs and the sleeves. Yet strange to say I had the feeling he was grown, for they did not seem as big as they should; in fact, though the arms of the coat was much too long, the shoulders was nearly fitting, so there was more breadth across his shoulders than I remembered. I wondered how old he was, and then who he was, and it made me angry to see him dressed so, pretending to be a gentleman, so I felt no fear of him. "That is you own doing, isn't it, sir," I said, very cold.

This pleased him. His face took on a look of amusement, almost natural, though there is something so wrong about him, simple pleasures is not in his range of expression. "Ever the serious moralist, aren't you Mary," he said. "And no pity in that hard heart for anyone who strays from your narrow little system of just deserts."

My temper flared the more, for I saw he had contempt for me. "How should I pity you?" I said.

"Why, I am run to the ground here," he replied. He looked around the yard, then down at his feet, which was on the edge of the garden. He took a step forward, so that he was standing on the hard dirt and I thought, he is right on my crocus, which was an odd thing to come to mind, but it did. He went on talking. "This yard is my last prison." He dug the toe of his boot into the soil. "I may as well dig up this strip of dirt and lie down in it. It would serve as well as a grave and I've no doubt everyone in this house would like to see me in it."

I looked at his boot as he spoke and then I looked up to his face and strange to say, he was so haggard and his eyes, though filled with rage, seemed also to be weary, full of pleading as well, and I thought, he is worn out from running. I could almost feel pity for him in that moment, as one feels pity for some dangerous animal what has caught his leg in a trap, so I did not want to help him for fear of my life, still it were no pleasure to see him struggle. I did not speak and he looked away at last, towards the house. "Will you tell them you have seen me?" he asked.

"Let me speak to my master," I said.

He fixed me with another of his dreadful sudden smiles, gone almost as soon as it come. "*I* am your master, Mary," he said. "Don't you know that yet?"

"Never," I said quickly. "That can never be. Let me speak to him and I'll do as he says. I will not take my orders from you."

My anger only amused him more and made him want to mock me, for he stepped back, holding his hands up as if he needed to defend himself against me. "What a temper, Mary," he said. "I'm sure he wouldn't approve. I can't let you see him unless you ask me proper." Then, while he stood sneering I fought down my feelings, which was all a mix of anger, pride and fear. "Please, sir," I said at last. "Let me see my master."

He frowned and that dark look come into his eyes which is so dangerous, bored and impatient and full of hatred, though why he should hate me I could not say.

Then he lifted his chin toward the theatre. "Very well," he said. "Lead the way."

I did not like to walk with him behind me and of course he followed so close I could hear his breath as clear as my own. When we got inside the theatre he reached up and caught me by my hair, which was loose, so I felt a sickness in my stomach and my knees went weak, for I thought, he has only brought me in here to kill me. He said, "This is far enough, Mary," so I stood still while he wound his hand tight through my hair. His other hand came around my throat and in a moment he had unfastened my cloak and pulled it back over one shoulder. I could not move for he had one hand at my throat and the other holding my head down, pulling my hair so tight I thought it would come out. He bent over my shoulder, pushing the sleeve of my shift aside with his mouth. Then I heard him draw in his breath so sharp it made a sound like a groan, and in the next second I felt his teeth sink into my shoulder, just at my neck, not hard at first but then very hard, so that I cried out. The pain was bad but my terror of what mun come next was worse and I felt my knees give out. His hand left my throat and his arm came about my waist, holding me up against him, but his teeth was still sunk in my shoulder, deeper and deeper until I thought they might meet over the bone. I could hardly see for the pain but I found my voice and said, "Please, sir. Do not do this."

He let me go all at once and I fell to my hands and knees on the floor. I did not move; from weakness and fear I could not. I listened to his breathing which was very loud and uneven, and in the big, cold theatre there was only that sound. "What prevents me from taking your life?" he asked, a strange question to put to me, so I thought he must be talking to himself. I did not move, and I felt his boot press into my side, trying to turn me over, but I kept still, my back to him, my face in my hands. He kicked me, but not hard, and said, "It is only that I've forgotten my knife." Then he walked to the steps that lead up to Master's cabinet and stood leaning against the railing, his back to me, nor did he speak. I sat up and rubbed my shoulder which was sore, but, I found, not bleeding, so I pulled my sleeve up and my cloak back over me.

"Wait here," he said and his voice was calm, though as it always is, harsh, so it seems he does not like to speak. "I'll send him down to you."

I got to my feet as he climbed the stairs. At the landing he stopped and took a key from his coat pocket. Then, without looking back at me, he turned it in the lock and let himself inside.

I stood in the dark theatre listening for the sound of voices but none came to me. I heard someone moving about but I could make out little from the sounds. There was no voices, but I thought I heard a clatter of a dish, and then a groan, though very weak. I wanted to see Master so hard my head ached and it was all I could do to stay where I was and not rush up the stairs and throw myself against the door. "If I could only see him," I said, but still he did not come. My eyes was quite used to the dark, so I looked about, trying to calm my fear by noting how nothing had changed. The boxes stood with their straw half pulled out, the same tools, covered with dust, was scattered on the floor, and in a beam of moonlight I could make out a fine cobweb stretched all across a corner of the windowpane. Nothing was disturbed. But, I thought, that is a lie. Everything is disturbed.

I heard a sound near the cabinet door, the handle turned and as the door opened a flood of light poured out, so for a moment my eyes was dazed and I could not see who was standing there. Then I saw it was Master, carrying the lamp in one hand and holding on to the stair rail with the other.

It was Master, but how changed. His shoulders was stooped and it was clear he clung to the rail for fear of falling down the stairs. He seemed all over smaller, thinner, his coat fell open at the collar and so did his shirt, as clothes do hang when they are too big. I could not make out his face clearly but I saw at once that it was gaunt, unshaven; his colour was not healthy but sallow and his beautiful silver hair lay flat and limp against his head, straying over his ears and his collar, for it had not been cut or combed. He came down the stairs slow and painful, mindful of nothing but the trouble to get down. When he was at the bottom, he held the lamp out before him and saw me standing in the darkness. "Mary," he said. "There you are."

"Oh, sir," I cried out. "Come back into the house with me this night. He is killing you."

"No, no," Master said, waving his hand before his eyes as if to brush away my words. "It is all my own doing." He sat down on the bottom step and put the lamp down at his feet. "I'll be fine in a moment. I'm just a little dizzy." He passed his hand across his face, then started at his own shadow, which the lamp had sent shooting up the wall so the movement of his hand had made a giant dark motion behind him. He laughed softly. "When you were a child, Mary," he said, "did you play shadow games?"

"No, sir," I said.

Master looked up at me, a smile still playing around his mouth. "Just as well," he said. "As it turns out, they can be very dangerous."

"Please, sir," I said. "I don't understand you."

Master held the lamp up before him and, moving his hand, made the shadow leap up again. He watched the shadow play but spoke to me. "How would you say we are related to our shadows, Mary?" he said. "If we cast them, are they not always part of us?"

"Sir," I said. "They are only a trick of the light."

Master put the lamp down on the step and fell to adjusting his cuffs, which was turned back. "It may be that *we* are the trick of the light, Mary," he said. "That has been the direction of my experiments. And I have been so successful, so marvellously successful. Why, no one would believe it." Then Master pulled himself to his feet by holding on to the rail. He took up the lamp and stood looking about the theatre, seeming pleased with all he saw. "What is the weather like outdoors, Mary?" he said.

"It's fine, sir," I said. "Clear and not cold. A fine night."

"Let us walk about the yard, then," he said. "It seems a long time since I've been out."

I agreed at once, thinking that the farther I got him from the cabinet, the closer he was to the house. He set the lamp back down on the floor and I followed him across the theatre to the door. When he stepped out onto the flags he took a deep breath, then looked about cheerfully. "Just as you promised, Mary," he said. "A beautiful night."

I fell into step beside him, thinking hard how best to persuade him, for he seemed in a strange way almost childish, so I did not know how to proceed.

He stopped after a few steps and gazed up at the stars. "You see," he said, "all blackness and only pin-points of light. Yet even if that is the truth about us, on such a night as this we can be glad we are alive."

Then I thought my poor Master had gone mad. He'd been shut up for weeks with a murderer and the strain had broken his mind. Still I could only reason with him, so I tried to take the course laid out for me. "As you value your life, sir," I said, "forget that man we have just left in your cabinet and come into the house."

Master looked down at me. "Now *he* is one who values his life," he said, as if it was a great accomplishment and would come as a surprise to me.

"I do not doubt that, sir," I said. "But he values no other. He has murdered one man that we know of. What is to keep him from murdering you?"

Master laughed. "He would not murder *me*," he said, as if the idea was not to be thought of.

"Sir," I protested, "he does not care for you."

"That is no matter," Master said. "He will not murder me. We are so bound up together he cannot. Nor can I walk across the yard and leave him behind, leave him to his fate. It isn't possible. God knows I wish it were."

"You are tired, sir," I said. "You may feel you haven't the strength . . ."

Master interrupted me. "It isn't a question of strength, Mary. Or even of will."

"Then what, sir?" I said.

"Pride, I suppose," Master said. "Pride got me into this, though pride of a different order. In that way Edward Hyde has liberated me, strange though it seems. I no longer care what the world thinks of me."

"Do you only care then for what *he* thinks of you?" I said.

Master frowned at this remark and I thought we both knew it was not my place to make it, yet I was past caring for what was proper, as it seemed to me Master's life hung in the balance. "Actually," Master said after a moment, "he does not think of me. Or if he does, it is only as the bandit recalls the cave that shelters him."

"How long can you shelter him?" I said. "How long before Mr. Poole spies him out, or your friends come to the very door in fear for your life?"

Master looked at me sadly. "Not much longer, Mary," he said.

"Then, sir," I pleaded. "Come into the house this

night and call the constables with me. You owe this man nothing and you have brought yourself to death's door trying to protect him."

"It's myself I'm trying to protect," Master said. His voice was very low and he stood with his face turned away from me so I could not see his expression. "It always has been. I care nothing for Edward Hyde."

Then a shudder come over him and he groaned, as he had that night in the library. I stepped toward him even as he reached out for me and I held him up, as I had before, looking into his eyes which seemed so strange and wild, I thought he could not see me. I could hear his teeth grinding in his jaws. His hand on my shoulder grew stronger, rather than weaker as I would have thought, and gripped me so hard it was all I could do not to cry out myself. Perhaps it was my fear for him, but as I struggled to hold him up his face seemed to change and his eyes grew dark with a look in them that was not like Master, but black and full of rage, and his lips, which was parted, seemed to swell and darken. Then the pain eased and his face grew pale. Drops of moisture gathered on his brow. His grip loosened on my shoulders and we stood apart. "He is impatient," Master said.

"Sir," I said, "is there nothing I can do to persuade you to come into the house with me?"

He stood gazing at me as if my words had no meaning to him. "How pale your face looks in the moonlight, Mary," he said. "I don't believe I've ever seen your hair loose like that."

"Please, sir," I said, but my voice was small and weak. He stepped close to me and put his arms about me. I rested my cheek against his shirt and closed my eyes. He held me so for a long moment while my heart was breaking and my eyes flooded over with tears. I felt his hands across my back and his mouth against my hair. "You do care for me," he said. "My dear girl. How I have come to trust you as I trust no other." When he released me I covered my face with my hands, for the tears were streaming down and I could not speak but only sob a word or two. "Please, sir," I said again. Master held me by my shoulders at arm's length. "As you care for me," he said, "keep this confidence. Tell no one what you have seen. It is the last request I will make of you."

I shook my head, no. "I cannot," I said. He took my chin in his hand and lifted my face so that he could look into it. "Mary," was all he said.

"I cannot," I said again. He smiled at me and brushed my hair back gently and I turned my face into his hand to kiss his fingers as they went by. Then while I stood, still sobbing, tears falling so I could not see and I knew I would not stop crying for many minutes to come, Master turned away from me and walked back to the theatre, going in at once and closing the door behind him.

Now as I write this, Annie is asleep, our house is quiet, but I will have no rest. All day I have made a show of working, but I could not say now even what I did, for I have my mind always across the yard where

Master is shut away from me, but not alone, as I am. I go over his words again and again, and feel his arms about me, his breath at my ear.

Where is my obligation? What do I owe my master? He asks for my silence, but how can I be silent if his life is in danger? And how can I make sense of the strange things he says to me, that he is bound up with this murderer in some way, that he would abandon him but cannot, that his pride has somehow brought him low and that, though he no longer cares for the world's opinion, it is himself he seeks to protect?

I can hardly breathe in this room, it feels so close. I know it is cold, but I cannot feel it, for it seems as if I am burning up, as if my blood is boiling. Even the candle casts a hot, reddish light on my page. I hear Master's voice and then the other—I cannot bear to hear it —saying, "*I* am your master. *I* am your master. Don't you know that yet?"

*M*aster was right. It did not last much longer. Four days passed and I did what I told him I could not do, I kept his confidence. Now I wonder was it right to do so. He left me in the yard believing I would do as he asked, even though I told him I could not, so it seems Master knows me better than I know myself.

All the next day the house was in a sorry way, for

Mr. Poole was sent running all over town in search of some chemical which was never the right one, for no sooner had he delivered it to the cabinet door then another order was thrown on the stairs. Master would hardly speak to him, but to say he must come to the steps every hour, so that no time would be wasted in having his orders filled. Mr. Poole told Cook something was not right and he did not like it, but could do nothing about it as he was always running. The breakfast tray came back untouched, but the lunch and dinner trays was empty, so Cook said at least he is eating, but I thought, one of them is eating but I doubt it is Master. Three days passed in this way. Then on Tuesday Cook told me Mr. Poole come into the kitchen after lunch looking as if he had run across town, though he'd only come across the yard. He sunk down in a chair and put his head down on the table. When Cook went to his side to see what ailed him she said he only turned his face towards her and said, "There is foul play." So she saw he'd had a shock and she made him a cup of tea, which he drank, hardly speaking, then said he'd gone into the theatre and surprised a man, not Master, digging about in the packing crates, looking for something. When the man saw Mr. Poole he let out a cry of fear and ran up the cabinet steps, closing the door behind him. Mr. Poole did not follow, for, he said, he was too stunned. He told Cook he'd felt something was amiss for many weeks now and this discovery had nearly broke his reason. Cook asked who was the man, but Mr. Poole said he hadn't seen him clear enough and could not say, only that he was a small man and very dark. So Cook said we mun call the constables but Mr. Poole did not like that plan and had another of his own, which was to go to Master's solicitor, Mr. Utterson, and tell him there could be no doubt Master was in some terrible danger if there had not already been foul play.

When I heard all this Mr. Poole was already gone for Mr. Utterson. Cook said it mun be Mr. Edward Hyde and no other, for he answers Mr. Poole's description, though he did not say it was him. I only nodded my head but said nothing and I thought, good then, it is not my doing but the business is found out and Master will be saved.

When I woke up I could not think where I was and it was many moments before the truth came to me, that Edward Hyde has killed himself and Master disappeared. This was the news Mr. Poole brought us after he and Mr. Utterson broke down the cabinet door to find the dying man gasping his last breath on the floor. And there was no doubt, Mr. Poole said, he was a self-destroyer, for he'd the empty bottle clutched in his hand and Mr. Utterson said he recognized the odour of the poison. So they searched for Master in the theatre and along the passage but he was not to be found, nor was there any way, as far as they could tell, he could have gone, for there was cobwebs clinging to every entry, all undisturbed, and they found the key to the passage broken on the flags on the street side of the door.

Then Mr. Utterson found a letter and a package of pages bound up, which was directed to him in Master's own hand. He told Mr. Poole he meant to take them away to study and that we was all to wait in the house, calling no one until a way to clear Master's name of any wrongdoing should reveal itself to Mr. Utterson.

So Mr. Poole come in and told us what they had found, though as he said, he could scarce believe his own eyes nor make any sense on it, but must have a hope that Mr. Utterson will return before morning and show us the way out of this mystery.

And that was all we knew, nor could we go out to the cabinet to see for ourselves but must make a show of eating dinner and clearing up. Annie and I went up to bed before the others, for I felt so anxious I wanted to lie in my bed and think what it all might mean. Then we lay down together and she said, "Where could our master have hid himself?" but before she'd puzzled out one answer she drifted off to sleep.

I thought I would not sleep but lay staring into the darkness, thinking of how I might find Master or he might send for me, for I could not believe he was lost to me. But somehow I did go to sleep and when I woke up it was a few moments before I knew what I was listening for, though the house was quiet all round me, and that was Master's step.

Of course he did not come.

Then I thought of Edward Hyde, or of his body, which lay still in the cabinet where he could harm no one, and as I thought of him I rubbed my shoulder which still is tender to me, though there was no marks upon it, and I seemed to hear his harsh voice in the dark room, saying he might as well dig a grave and lay himself in it, so I thought, that is just what he has done, for he feared the sure steps to the gallows more than death itself.

Yet I could scarce believe it. Such a man does not take his own life, but howls for mercy once he knows he can only expect to die if he calls for justice, and fights for his life to the last moment.

A strange fear come to me, so strong that I sat up in the bed holding the cover to my chest and that was this, he is not dead. I seemed to hear his footsteps, that light, halting way he has, pacing back and forth, as Mr. Poole said he did before they broke open the door, back and forth in my own head until I could bear it no longer and got out of the bed.

I must see for myself, I thought, but how was I to do it, for Mr. Poole would be waiting up for Mr. Utterson's return, so I must get past him to get the key to the theatre, and then I would run the risk that they might come out behind me. Still, I thought, it could be done, for Mr. Poole would be in the front hall so I had only to get down the back stairs past the ground floor and if I moved quietly in the kitchen he would not be likely to hear me. I pulled my cloak over my shift and went out onto the landing, listening for any sound that might give me away. I made my way down the stairs one at a time, pausing every step and scarce breathing, for it seemed my own breath was loud in my ears. I could see little but my own bare foot as I looked down, and I remembered the night Master had smiled to see I went about the house without my boots. Pray, I thought, he may smile to see this foot again.

In this way I arrived at the kitchen, where everything was quiet and orderly and I knew my way so well I did not need a light. I stopped at the pantry and took the key to the theatre from the nail, then slipped out the back door to the yard.

It was a clear, cold, windy night and overhead there was a few thin clouds moving along swiftly as if they was being drawn across the sky on a string. My hair blew wild about my face, so I had to be constantly pushing it away from my eyes with one hand while with my other I held my cloak in close about me. The flags was like ice against my feet and I stepped lightly upon them, hurrying past the garden where I noted the tips of the bulbs have broken through the soil. I did not pause but struggled on against the wind to the theatre door where, with some difficulty, I got the key in the lock. The wind caught the door and threw it open with such force it nearly knocked me down, but I clung to it and pulled myself inside, hauling the door back in with me. Then I could not hear the wind and it seemed the whole world had suddenly gone very still and black. I did not move but something moved inside me and that was a stab of fear, sudden and deep, like a flash of light. I could make out the staircase across the theatre, rising up into a blackness deeper than the one in which I stood. And if I climb those stairs, I thought, and light the lamp, if I look on his dead body, if I touch him and know he is cold and truly gone and Master must be safe somehow, then will this fear be laid to rest?

And strange to say it come to me that I was more afraid to look on Edward Hyde dead than I was to see him alive. So I reasoned with myself, you have come this far, you must see it through, and I took a step forward, and then another, halting at each one, my ears straining for a sound, my eyes for any movement in the room, and as I drew closer to the staircase it seemed my heart was pressed so tight against my chest I could not get my breath. I clutched the rail and dragged myself up a few steps, thinking of how Master looked that night he come down to speak to me, which was the last time I saw him, so weak and his manner so strange. If only, I thought, the door would open and he would come out to me now. But in a moment I knew that was not possible for I found the door and it could never be opened properly again. Mr. Poole told Cook he had hacked it open with an axe while Edward Hyde cried out for mercy on the other side, so I had imagined the lock giving way, but the hinges had come free as well and the panel was split in two.

They had propped the wreck of it up against the doorway, only to cover the space a little, for it was easy enough to slip past it on one side, so it served no use in keeping anyone in nor out. I pressed against the wall, pulling my cloak in tight around me. I could see nothing ahead of me, for the curtains was drawn so even the dim light of the moon could not get in, and I shuddered as I took the first step, fearing my bare foot might find his body before my hands could find the lamp. So I crouched down and made my way with my hands outstretched, feeling the carpet before me. I come to the back of the chair before the fireplace and groped my way around it to the tiles where I felt along the edge to the matchbox. I took out a few and set at once to striking one against the grate, but my hands was shaking so bad I only wore off the tip of the first one. The blackness seemed to press in tight all about me and I looked and looked to see through it, so that I began to see spots of colour swirling about, while I struck the second match once, then again, full of panic and thinking, when it lit, would I find I was looking down into his dead eyes? On the third try it took and I breathed a great sigh of relief, cupping my hand round the little flame and standing up at once to bring it to the lamp. No sooner was I up than I felt a movement at my shoulder, so that I gasped, whirling around where I stood, for he was standing just behind me. But it was my own reflection I found gazing back at me, open-mouthed, from the cheval glass, my hair standing out wild around my face, my eyes filled with terror while the match flared a little, then faded. As quick as I could I took a new one and lit it from the other. Still, my hands was shaking so bad and my palms had gone damp, so it was all I could do to bring the two sticks together. Then I held my hand up to find the lamp, which stood on the table nearby, the wick neatly trimmed and the glass as clean as if I'd done it myself. I used another match to get to it, then with what relief I saw the wick take the flame and a rosy glow come up all around me. Now the sitting room came to life before me and I saw it had been left in perfect order, even to the tea things laid out neatly on the sideboard, and there was no sign of anyone living or dead upon the carpet. So I knew he must be in the part of the room where the laboratory table was, which was behind me. I turned in my place very slow, trying somehow to brace myself against what must leap out at my eyes.

There was the table, littered with strange bottles and glasses, some with coloured liquid standing in them still, as if Master had just stepped away from an experiment a moment ago. I held the lamp up so that I might see farther, but my own shadow fell across the table and quenched the ugly glimmering of the bottles there. Then I seemed to hear Master say, If we cast our shadows, are they not always part of us?

I felt a queer sickness in my stomach and I swallowed hard once, then again, for as I stood gazing at the table it was as if the pieces of some wicked puzzle fell into place before my eyes. His experiments, I thought, and I heard Master say he had been successful, so successful no one would believe him. Then I lowered the lamp and as I did I saw him. He had fallen on the far side of the table, near the window. Perhaps he thought to get out that way. He lay on his back, his hand stretched out towards me, clutching the empty bottle as Mr. Poole had said. My heart lurched in my chest and I felt a gagging at my throat as if that hand was closed about it. The sleeve was rolled well back on the shirt, and as I approached I saw the trouser legs rolled up from his ankles as well. I knew what I would find as I rounded the table, and I clutched the end of it to hold me up. I raised the lamp to see his face, which was not as I had ever seen it but all twisted in a grimace of pain, the lips stretched cruelly over the gritted teeth, his eyes wide open and staring, so that he seemed to call out to me for help.

I set the lamp upon the table where it made a great clatter of light among the bottles and tubes there and I remembered the first time I come into this room so long ago and how I set my heart against it, so even then I must have known. All the time the truth was right before my eyes and especially that last night when I held Master up in the yard and saw the change come upon his face, and those other eyes looking out at me for a moment, but I would not understand, as if I was too stubborn to know it.

How many times did he tell me?

But Master was right, who would believe it? How could one man be two—one kind, gentle, generous, the other with no care but his own pleasure and no pleasure but the suffering of his fellows?

I leaned upon the table and glared at the bottles, all glittering before me, and wanted to smash them but I had no strength. Indeed my knees no longer held me up so I slipped to the floor. Then I crawled to Master, speaking to him softly. His face was turned towards mine, his silver hair matted about it in a way I did not like to see, and his eyes, so wide and staring, seemed to look through my head at the table behind me. From the yard I could hear the sound of heavy footsteps and raised voices crossing to the theatre. They were coming to take him away, take him from me entire, and they knew—now everyone would know—my gentle Master and Edward Hyde was one and the same. "But you said you no longer care for the world's opinion," I said to him, "nor will I." When I reached him I kissed his hand, as I did that night in the yard, then I tried to pry the bottle from him, for I did not like to see it, but his fingers was stiff, he held on with death's own grip. "This is a cruel trick," I said to Master. "That he should take his own life and leave you behind to answer for it." I smoothed his hair back away from his forehead, but I did not try to close his eyes.

I heard the footsteps crossing the theatre; soon they would be on the stairs. "Well, let them come," I said and I lay down beside Master, covering us both with my cloak as best I could, for the floor was cold. I rested my head upon his chest and put my arms about his neck. I could hear my own heart in my ear and it seemed to be beating against his still one.

That was how they found us.

AFTERWORD

The preceding extraordinary diaries came to light three years ago in a transferral of property at Bray, in Berkshire, west of London. How they arrived in my hands is a complicated story, though not a surprising one, as I have long had an interest in old letters and diaries and am well known to those who deal in such documents. The diaries (my own term; Mary Reilly referred to her writings as "journals") were in four leatherette notebooks, (6¼" by 8½", lined pages, 20 to 21 lines per page) closely written and containing a few pages separate and folded, the principal being the account with which I have chosen to begin Mary Reilly's story. Mary's habitual frugality shows in her method of writing, which was to put two lines above the top line on each page and another two below the last, so that the page is entirely covered.

The inside covers of the books are lined with marbled paper and the photograph, the traditional *carte* of the period, is pasted into the inside cover of the first book, the text of which is not included here, for reasons I will explain, and I presume it to be of Mary Reilly herself.

I have taken various liberties with Mary's text to prepare it for publication, and these should be explained so that the reader will have a better sense of the original manuscript. First, as I have indicated, I have omitted one of the surviving volumes. That is Mary's account of her life at Mrs. Torbay's house, her first position, which predated the text presented here by some years. Mary was probably fifteen or sixteen at the time and her style is less developed, her observations less acute, and her obsession with people being in their proper places—which we here see put to the test so poignantly—at its most full-blown and defensive. The Torbay house was a crowded one, with five children and a large staff. Mary was the lowest of these and she was under the influence of a lady's maid named Mrs. Swit (whom she refers to in the present text), who filled her head with maxims about the proper relations of servants to masters and, importantly for our sake, encouraged Mary to keep a record of her life. If the text here presented creates, as I hope it will, an active interest in this serious and strangely eloquent young woman, her adolescent efforts may be published at a later date.

Because Mary did not date her entries, it is difficult to tell how much time is covered in the three books I have transcribed. Considering the amount of work that fell to her, it would be surprising if she had had the energy to write every day. Sometimes she begins by describing a passage of days, at other times she simply says "yesterday," or "today," which allows for the possibility that many days have passed. The space breaks between entries are entirely my own creation; Mary did not waste paper by leaving even a line unfilled. I have made no effort to compact the three books; they stand as she left them.

I have also taken great liberties with Mary's punctuation and spelling. She rarely used punctuation at all and her method of capitalizing proper names was erratic, though it is interesting to note that she always failed to capitalize the word "i" and never failed to capitalize the word "Master." She used dashes occasionally as commas and left off all possessive apostrophes. She recorded dialogue without breaks in the line or marks of any kind. All of these idiosyncrasies I have standardized for ease in reading.

I have retained, however, Mary's habitual misuse of the verb "to be" as it seems characteristic of her voice, as is her use of the dialect "mun" for "must." Occasional words were illegible; these I have substituted with the most logical option. Mary sometimes names places and streets with one letter followed by a dash, for example in "H———." I have retained this peculiarity.

Mary's diaries break off abruptly and the last book is not like the others filled. Given the compromising situation in which she was discovered (even by contemporary standards, a domestic found late at night in her nightgown embracing her dead employer might expect repercussions), it seems probable that she did not leave Jekyll's house with that document most vital to the Victorian servant, that passport from hardship and squalor to the haven of domestic servitude: a good "character."

However, as Mary shows herself throughout her chronicle to be a resourceful and honest young woman, as well as a better than average servant, we can surmise that she recovered from the shock of her master's suicide and landed on her feet in some less fantastic household.

The question of what really happened to Mary's employer, Henry Jekyll, is not so easily resolved. It is difficult to credit Mary's own conclusion, that her beloved Dr. Jekyll and his murderous assistant Edward Hyde were one and the same person, but not for the reasons Mary gives us: "How could one man be two, one kind, gentle, generous, the other with no care but his own pleasure and no pleasure but the suffering of his fellows?" A glance at the daily newspapers will remind us that such duplicity is not uncommon, especially among those who set themselves up as moral arbiters among us. One need only examine the lives of the wife, children and secretary of many a reformer to uncover sufficient duality of purpose to fill a column, sometimes a book. What is unexplained and incomprehensible in Henry Jekyll's case is the physical transformation, which, if we are to believe Mary's account, was considerable, and given Mr. Poole's panic driven search for a certain chemical as well as Jekyll's own remarks about his experiments, was achieved by the administration of some drug.

I propose two possible solutions. There may be others. The first is that Mr. Poole and Mr. Utterson lied about what they found in the cabinet, that they knew Jekyll had killed himself, possibly from despair over his addiction to some drug (Edward Hyde might easily have been his supplier and have disappeared after the murder of Sir Danvers Carew, leaving Jekyll to bedevil chemists who were unable to provide him with a sufficient or pure supply) and that, in order to buy time to save Jekyll's name, they concocted the story of the dead Hyde. This may seem farfetched, nor does it explain the reappearance of Edward Hyde the night of Jekyll's death, but Mr. Poole and Mr. Utterson show themselves to be obsessed with the good name of Henry Jekyll, and the shock of breaking down a door to find they had themselves driven the poor man to suicide could have caused them to make up a story which, in the end, would cause more trouble than it was worth. If this was the case it would explain the movement of the boot, which Mary comments upon after Dr. Jekyll's fall in the yard. If Dr. Jekyll and Edward Hyde were not the same person, Hyde might easily have come into the yard and moved the boot. It seems entirely within his character to play such a pointless joke.

A second possibility is that Mary is correct and that Henry Jekyll did somehow come upon a way of transforming himself into the thoroughly unrecognizable and reprehensible Edward Hyde. That this involved losing a foot or so in height, a total change of features and coloring, as well as a stripping away of the effects of age (for all who see him agree that Hyde is small and young) strains credulity, but surely Jekyll would have found the transformation of dots of light into moving pictures, which we enjoy without astonishment, equally as incredible. The experiment, begun out of curiosity by the kindly, aging philanthropist, must then gradually have gotten out of control, requiring more and more of the chemical to effect the transformation back into Jekyll, until at last no amount would do. It does seem clear, and rather sad as well, that Jekyll closed himself up in his cabinet in a state of despair, knowing that he could no longer keep Edward Hyde at bay. To share one's body with a dangerous criminal is not a fate anyone would willingly embrace, but to share one's consciousness as well, which it seems was in some degree Jekyll's unhappy condition, this must be terror indeed. The curious psychological relationship of Dr. Jekyll to Edward Hyde might be best explained by some student of human psychology adept at untangling the complex threads that so loosely knit the conscious to the unconscious. It is a mysterious connection and one that would surely repay study, for who among us has not felt at some moment the press of an unconscious desire to create havoc? Is it not the fear of this impluse that drives us to insist upon social order?

A third and final mystery which also might entertain a scholar more pertinacious than myself is the manner by which Mary's diaries traveled from London to Bray. There are several possibilities, one of which I should mention, though only because it is bound to be raised by someone who believes, as a librarian at the British Museum assured me, that such a diary as this could not exist because housemaids in the late Victorian period were all illiterate.

We have a fair amount of evidence that this was not the case. Many such diaries have survived, as well as an account of an underhousemaid in London who published a novel, the subject of which was her employer's family, thereby creating a scandal, and undoubtedly a good deal of anxiety in many an upper-class household. This, of course, raises a specter over the present manuscript, one which I neither endorse nor seek to discredit, and that is the possibility that the sad and disturbing story unfolded for us in the pages of Mary's diaries is now and always was intended to be nothing less serious than a work of fiction.

About the Author

Valerie Martin is the author of *The Consolation of Nature*, *A Recent Martyr*, *Alexandra*, *Set in Motion*, and *Love*. Born in Missouri and raised in New Orleans, she has taught at the University of New Orleans, the University of Alabama, New Mexico State University, and Mount Holyoke College. She lives in Montague, Massachusetts, and currently teaches in the graduate writing program at the University of Massachusetts.